❧ SOCIETY WEDDINGS ❧

Rocco Mondelli and Olivia Fitzgerald

*invite you to celebrate their union
as they become husband and wife.*

*7 o'clock in the evening
April 2015
The Mondelli Estate, Lake Como*

dinner & dancing to follow

**...but only if Rocco can win back
his runaway bride!**

SOCIETY WEDDINGS

Dedicated bachelors Rocco Mondelli, Christian Markos, Stefan Bianco and Zayed Al Afzal met and bonded at university, wreaking havoc among the female population. In the decade since graduating they've made their marks on the worlds of business and pleasure, becoming wealthy and powerful.

Marriage was never something Rocco, Christian, Stefan or Zayed were ever after...but things change, and now they'll have to do whatever it takes to get themselves to the church on time!

Yet nothing is as easy as it seems...and the women these four have set their sights on have plans of their own!

Your embossed invitation is in the mail and you are cordially invited to

The marriage of *Rocco Mondelli & Olivia Fitzgerald*
April 2015

The marriage of *Christian Markos & Alessandra Mondelli*
May 2015

The marriage of *Stefan Bianco & Clio Norwood*
June 2015

The marriage of *Sheikh Zayed Al Afzal & Princess Nadia Amani*
July 2015

*So RSVP and get ready to enjoy
the pinnacle of luxury and opulence
as the world's sexiest billionaires
finally say "I do."*

Jennifer Hayward

The Italian's Deal for I Do

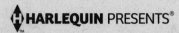

HARLEQUIN PRESENTS®

Special thanks and acknowledgment are given to
Jennifer Hayward for her contribution
to the Society Weddings series.

ISBN-13: 978-0-373-13329-1

The Italian's Deal for I Do

First North American Publication 2015

Copyright © 2015 by Harlequin Books S.A.

Recycling programs
for this product may
not exist in your area.

Printed in U.S.A.

Jennifer Hayward has been a fan of romance since filching her sister's novels to escape her teenage angst. Her career in journalism and PR, including years of working alongside powerful, charismatic CEOs and traveling the world, has provided perfect fodder for the fast-paced, sexy stories she likes to write, always with a touch of humor. A native of Canada's east coast, Jennifer lives in Toronto with her Viking husband and young Viking-in-training.

Books by Jennifer Hayward

Harlequin Presents

The Magnate's Manifesto
Changing Constantinou's Game

The Delicious De Campos
The Divorce Party
An Exquisite Challenge
The Truth About De Campo

Visit the Author Profile page
at Harlequin.com for more titles.

To my editor Laura McCallen and fellow authors Michelle Smart, Andie Brock and Tara Pammi who made the Columbia Four such a joy to write. *Memento vivere!*

And for Valentina and your invaluable help with the beautiful Italian language. *Grazie!*

CHAPTER ONE

"HE WILL NOT make it through the night."

The grizzled old priest had served almost a century of Mondellis in the lakeside village of Varenna. He rested his gnarled, weathered hand on the ornately carved knob of the inches-thick, dark-stained door of Giovanni Mondelli's bedroom and nodded toward the patriarch's two grandchildren. "You must say your goodbyes. Leave nothing unsaid."

His gravelly tone was somber, weighted with the grief of an entire village. It cut through Rocco Mondelli like a knife, severing a lifeline, rendering him incapable of speech. Italian fashion icon Giovanni Mondelli, son of the Italian people, had been the father he'd never had. He'd been Rocco's guiding influence when he'd taken his grandfather's place as CEO of House of Mondelli and brought it kicking and screaming into the twenty-first century. Transformed it into a revered global couture powerhouse.

He could not be losing him.

Rocco's heart sputtered to a stop, then came back to life in a brutal staccato that pounded against the walls of his chest. Giovanni was everything to him. Father, mentor, friend... He wasn't ready to let him go. Not yet.

His sister, Alessandra, grasped his arm, her knuckles white against the dark material of his suit. "I—I don't think I can do this," she stumbled huskily, her glossy brown hair tangled around her face, eyes wide. "It's too sudden. I have too much to say."

Rocco ignored the desire to throw himself on the floor and cry out that it wasn't fair, like he had at age seven when he'd stood on the deck of a boat outside this window on Lake Como in a miniature-size suit, his big, brown eyes trained on his *papa* as he tossed his mother's ashes into the brilliant blue water. Life wasn't fair. It had nothing to do with fair. It had given him Alessandra, but it had taken away his beloved mother. Never could that be considered a fair compromise.

He turned and gripped his sister by the shoulders, breathing through the searing pain that gripped his chest. "We can and we will, because we have to, *sorella*."

Tears streamed down Alessandra's face, negotiating the crevices of her stubborn mouth. "I can't, Rocco. I won't."

"You *will*." He pulled her into his arms and rested his chin on her head. "Gather your thoughts. Think of what you need to say. There isn't much time."

Alessandra soaked his shirt with silent tears. It had always been Rocco's job as much as it had been Giovanni's to hold this family together following the death of his mother and his father's subsequent descent into gambling and drink. But he did not feel up to it now. He felt as though one of the breezes wafting in from the lake might fell him with a single, innocent, misplaced nudge. But giving in to weakness, into emotion, had never been an option for him.

He set Alessandra away from him and slid an arm around her shoulders to support her slight weight. His gaze went to the short, balding doctor standing behind the priest. "Is he awake?"

The doctor nodded. "Go now."

His strong, sometimes misguided, but always confident sister trembled underneath his fingers as he led her into Giovanni's bedroom. If the saying was true you could smell death in the air, it was not the case here. He could *feel* the warmth, the vital energy Giovanni Mondelli had worn like a second skin. That he had infused into every single one of his designs. He could *hear* the caustic bite of his grandfather's laughter before it turned rich and chiding and full of wisdom. *Smell* the spicy, sophisticated scent that clung to every piece of clothing he wore.

It was Rocco's eyes, however, that stripped him of any shred of hope. The sight of his all-powerful grandfather lost in a sea of white sheets, his vibrant olive skin devoid of color, snared his breath in his chest. This was not Giovanni.

He swallowed past the fist in his throat. "Go," he urged Alessandra, pushing her forward.

Alessandra climbed onto the massive bed and wrapped her slim arms around her grandfather. The sight of Giovanni's eyes watering was too much for Rocco to bear. He turned away, walked to the window and stared out at the lake.

He and Alessandra had flown the fifty kilometers from the House of Mondelli headquarters in Milan via helicopter as soon as they had heard the news. But his stubborn grandfather had been ignoring pains in his chest all day, and by the time they'd got here, there was little the doctors could do.

His mouth twisted. If he knew his grandfather, he'd probably decided this was the cleanest way to go. Giovanni Mondelli was not beyond manipulating the world to his advantage. What better way to go out then in a blaze of glory on the eve of Mondelli's greatest fall line ever?

But then again, Rocco conceded, Giovanni had been ready to join his beloved wife, Rosa, in the sweet afterlife, as he called it, for almost twenty years. He had lived life to the fullest, refused to fade after her passing, but there had been a part of him that yearned for her with every waking breath.

He would have her back, he'd promised.

Alessandra let out a sob and rushed from the room. Rocco strode to the bed, his gaze settling on his grandfather's pale face. "You've broken her heart."

"Sandro did that a long time ago," his grandfather said wearily, referring to Rocco's father, who Alessandra had been named for. His eyes fluttered as he patted the bed beside him. "Sit."

Rocco sat, swallowed hard. "Nonno, I need to tell you…"

His grandfather laid his wrinkled, elegant, long-fingered hand over his. "I know. *Ti amo, mio figlio.* You have become a great man. Everything I knew you could be."

The lump in Rocco's throat grew too large for him to forge past.

His grandfather fixed his dark eyes on him, staring hard in an act of will to keep them open. "Trust yourself, Rocco. Trust the man you've become. Understand why I've done the things I've done."

His eyes fluttered closed. Rocco's heart slammed against his chest. "Giovanni, it is not your time."

His grandfather's eyes slitted open. "Promise me you will take care of Olivia."

"Olivia?" Rocco frowned in confusion.

His grandfather's eyes fluttered closed. Stayed closed this time. A fist reached inside Rocco's chest and clamped down hard on his heart. He took his grandfather's shoulders in his hands and shook them hard. *Come back. Do not leave me.* But Giovanni's eyes remained shut.

The spirit of the House of Mondelli, the flame that had burned passion into brilliant, groundbreaking collections for fifty years, into his own heart, was extinguished.

Rocco let out a primal roar and rested his forehead against his grandfather's lined brow.

"No," he whispered over and over again. It was too soon.

* * *

The emotion he had exhibited upon the death of his grandfather was nowhere to be seen in the week following as Rocco negotiated the mind-numbing details of organizing Giovanni's funeral, now reaching state-like proportions, and the settlement of his estate. The Mondelli holdings were vast, with properties and business interests spanning the globe. Even with his own intimate knowledge of the company and its entities, it would take time.

Alessandra helped him plan the funeral. Everyone, it seemed, wanted to come—public and government figures, heads of state and celebrities Giovanni had dressed over his forty-five years in the business. Weeding them out was their challenge.

And, of course, the remainder of the Columbia Four were coming: the three men Rocco had met and bonded with during their first week at Columbia University. Not a mean feat given the intense, grueling schedules of Christian Markos, Stefan Bianco and Zayed Al Afzal. Athens-born Christian was a financial whiz kid and deal maker who divided his time between Greece and Hong Kong. The inscrutable Sicilian, Stefan Bianco, preferred to make his millions masterminding the world's biggest real-estate deals on his private jet rather than in his hometown of Manhattan, but then again everyone knew Stefan had commitment issues. The final member of the group, Sheikh Zayed Al Afzal, would have the longest to travel from his home in the heart of the Arabian desert—a tiny country named Gazbiyaa.

It comforted him as he sat down with the Mondelli family's longtime lawyer, Adamo Donati, to review Giovanni's will, to know the men he considered more brothers than friends would be by his side. The bond he shared with those men was inviolate. Impenetrable. Built from years of knowing one another's inner thoughts. And although his life was not the only one that was tumultuous at the moment, his friends would not miss such an important event, including Zayed, whose country was embroiled in rising tensions with a neighboring kingdom and teetering on the verge of war.

Memento vivere was the Columbia Four's code. Remember to live. Which meant living big, risking big and always having one another's back.

"Shall we begin?"

Adamo, Giovanni's sage sixty-five-year-old longtime friend, who was not only a brilliant lawyer but a formidable business brain, tilted his chin at him in an expectant look. Rocco nodded and focused his attention on the lawyer. "Go ahead."

Adamo glanced down at the papers in front of him. "In terms of the properties, Giovanni has split them between you and Alessandra. I'm sure this is no surprise, as you've talked to him about it. Alessandra will receive the house in St. Barts and the apartment in Paris, while you will take ownership of Villa Mondelli and the house in New York."

Rocco inclined his head. Alessandra, a world-class photographer who traveled the world doing shoots, had always joked Villa Mondelli was too big for her, that she'd rattle around its sprawling acres by herself, while it was the only place on earth Rocco felt he could truly breathe.

He cocked a brow at the lawyer. "My father?"

"The current arrangement will continue. Giovanni left a sum of money in Sandro's name for you to administer."

Like a child unable to manage his own pocket money. Rocco had long given up on the idea that his father could manage anything, but he wondered if somewhere inside him he was waiting for the day Sandro would apologize for gambling away their family home. For handing them over to Giovanni when he could no longer cope. That someday he might step forward and shock them all. Until then, his father had been provided with an apartment in the city, a weekly shipment of groceries and a limited amount of spending money that inevitably went to gambling rather than to his own personal grooming.

When that ran out, he would slink back asking for more, and when he was told no, he did things like showing up drunk and disheveled at Alessandra's twenty-fifth birthday party, embarrassing them all.

Mouth set, he gestured for Adamo to continue.

The lawyer looked down at the papers. "There is another apartment in Milan. Giovanni purchased it a year ago. It is not accounted for in the will."

"Another apartment?" Rocco frowned. His grandfather had never liked to stay in the city. He preferred to drive to the villa each day or take the company helicopter.

The lawyer's olive skin took on a ruddy hue, his gaze glancing off Rocco as he looked up. "It's in Giovanni's name, but a woman has been living there. I had someone look into it. Her name is Olivia Fitzgerald."

Rocco sucked in a breath. "Olivia Fitzgerald, the model?"

"We think so. It took some digging. She's not using her real name."

He stared at Adamo as if he'd just told him the Pope was turning Protestant. Olivia Fitzgerald, one of the world's top supermodels, signed to a competitor five years ago and unattainable to the House of Mondelli, had dropped off the face of the earth a year ago. Hadn't worked a day since, reneging on a three-million-dollar contract with a French cosmetics company. And Giovanni had been keeping her in an apartment in this city? While the tabloids scoured the earth for her...

His gaze met the lawyer's as he came to the inevitable conclusion.

"He was involved with her."

Adamo's cheeks flushed even darker. "In some way, yes. The neighbors say he spent time with her in the apartment. They were seen arm in arm, going for dinner."

Rocco pressed his hands to his temples. Giovanni, his seventy-year-old grandfather, had taken a twenty-something-year-old mistress? One of the world's great supermodels… A party girl extraordinaire who'd apparently frittered her way out of her million-dollar bank balances as fast as she'd filled them. It seemed preposterous. Was he even living on the same planet he had been a week ago?

Promise me you will take care of Olivia.

Cristo. It was true. Blood rushed through his head, pulsing at his temples. As if he would continue to allow his grandfather's former lover to live on Mondelli property now that Giovanni was gone. A woman who had taken up with him in a transparent attempt to avail herself of his fortune.

He leveled a look at the lawyer. "Give me what you have on her. I'll deal with Olivia Fitzgerald."

Adamo nodded. Ran a hand over his balding head and gave him another of those hesitant looks, so uncharacteristic of him.

Rocco arched a brow. "*Per favore*, tell me there are no more mistresses."

A faint smile crossed Adamo's lips. "Not that I know of."

"Then, what? Spit it out, Adamo."

The lawyer's smile faded. "Giovanni has left you a fifty percent stake of House of Mondelli, Rocco. The remaining ten percent controlling stake has been allocated to Renzo Rialto to manage until he sees fit to turn it over."

Rocco blinked. Attempted to digest. Giovanni hadn't left him a controlling stake in Mondelli? Prior to his grandfather's death, the Mondelli family had held a 60 percent share in the company, with outside shareholders holding the remaining 40 percent, leaving the family firmly in control of the legendary fashion retailer. Giving him the power he had needed as CEO to guide Mondelli forward. Why would Giovanni have taken that power out of his hands and given it to Renzo Rialto, the chairman of the board, who had always been Rocco's nemesis?

Adamo read his dismay. "He didn't want you to feel overwhelmed without him. He wants you to be able to lean on the board for support. Find your feet. When the board feels you're ready, they'll hand over the remaining shares."

"Find my feet?" White-hot rage sliced through him, rage that had been building since his grandfather's death. Steel edged, it straightened every limb, singed every nerve ending, until it escaped out his fingertips as he slapped his palms down on the desk and brought himself eye to eye with the lawyer. "I have built this company into something *Giovanni* could never have envisioned. Taken it from prosperous to *wildly successful.* I don't need to find my feet, Adamo. I need what's rightfully mine—control of this company."

Adamo lifted a hand in a placating gesture. "You have to consider your personal history, Rocco. You have been a renegade. You have not listened to the advice the board has tried to give you."

"Because it was *wrong.* They wanted to keep Mondelli languishing in its past glory when it was clear it needed to move with the times."

"I agree." Adamo shrugged. "But not everyone felt that way. There is a great deal of conservatism within the board, a nostalgic desire not to strip away what made the company great. You're going to need to use more finesse to work your way through this one."

The blood in his head tattooed a rhythm against his skull. *Finesse?* The only thing that worked with the board was to whack them over the head with a big stick before they all retired in a wave of self-important glory.

Adamo eyed him. "There is also your personal life. You are not what the board considers a stable, secure guiding figure for Mondelli."

Rocco reared his head back. "Do not go there, Adamo."

"It was a…delicate situation."

"The one where the board castrated me for an affair I didn't even know I was having?"

"She was a judge's wife. There was a child."

"Not mine." He practically yelled the words at Adamo. "The DNA is in."

"Not before the entire affair caused Mondelli some considerable political difficulties." Adamo pinned him with a stern look of his own. "You weren't careful enough about which playgrounds you chose to dip into, Rocco. You play too fast and easy sometimes, and the board doesn't like it. They particularly worry now that Giovanni isn't here to guide you."

So his grandfather had thought it a good idea to handcuff him to the chairman of the board? To assign him a *babysitter*? He eyed the lawyer, his temper dangerously close to exploding. "I am CEO of the House of Mondelli. I do not need guiding. I need for a woman to *tell me* when she's still married. And if you think I'm going to sit around while the board rubber stamps my every decision, you and they are out of your minds."

Adamo gave a fatalistic lift of his shoulder. "The will is airtight. You have a fifty-percent share. The only person who can give you control is Renzo Rialto."

Renzo Rialto. A difficult, self-important boar of a man who had been a lifelong friend of Giovanni's, but never a huge fan of him personally, even though he couldn't fault what he'd done with the bottom line.

He would relish pushing Rocco's buttons.

He scraped his chair back, stood and paced to the window. Burying his hands in his pockets, he looked down at Via della Spiga, the most famous street in Milan where the House of Mondelli couture collection flew out the door of the Mondelli boutique at five hundred euros apiece. *This* was the epicenter of power. The playground he had commanded so magnificently since his father had defected from life and his path had been chosen.

He would not be denied his destiny.

And yet, he thought, staring sightlessly down at the stream of chicly dressed shoppers with colorful bags in their hands, his grandfather was making him pay for the aggressive business manner that had made Mondelli a household name. For an error in judgment, a carelessness with women that had never *once* interfered with his ability to do his job.

Understand why I've done the things I've done... Giovanni's dying words echoed into his head. Was this what he'd been talking about? And how did it fit with everything else he'd said? *You have become a great man... Trust the man you've become.*

It made no sense.

Anger mingled with grief so heavy, so all encompassing, he leaned forward and rested his palms on the sill. Did this have to do with his father's legacy? Had Sandro made his grandfather gun-shy of handing over full responsibility of the company he'd built despite Rocco's track record? Did he imagine he, as Sandro's flesh and blood, was capable of the same self-combustion?

He turned and looked at the lawyer. "I am *not* my father."

"No, you aren't," Adamo agreed calmly. "But you do like to enjoy yourself with that pack of yours."

Rocco scowled. "The reports of our partying are highly overblown."

"The women part is not. You forget I've known you since you were in *pannolino*, Rocco."

He crooked a brow at him. "What would you have me do? Marry one of them?"

Adamo held his gaze. "It would be the smartest thing you could do. Show you have changed. Show you are serious about putting Mondelli first. Marry one of those connected Italian woman you love to date and become a stable family man. You might even find you like it."

Rocco stared at him. He was serious. *Dio.* Not *ever* happening. He'd seen what losing his mother had done to his father, what losing Rosa had done to Giovanni. He didn't need that kind of grief in his life. He had enough responsibility keeping this company, this family, afloat.

"I would not hold my breath waiting for the silk-covered invitation," he advised drily. "Do you have any more bombshells for me, or can I pay Renzo Rialto a visit?"

"A few more items of note."

They went through the immediate to-dos. Rocco picked up his messages after that, went to his car and headed to Rialto's offices. The retired former CEO of a legendary Italian brand was a thorn in his side, but manage him he would.

He swung the yellow limited edition Aventador, his favorite material possession, onto a main artery, attempting to corral his black temper along the way. He would deal with Rialto, then he would take care of the other complication in his life. Olivia Fitzgerald was about to find her very fine rear end out on the streets of Milan. Just as soon as he found out what kind of game she was playing.

CHAPTER TWO

ROCCO HAD EXPECTED Olivia Fitzgerald to be beautiful. She had, after all, a face that had launched a dozen brands to stardom. A toned, curvaceous body that regularly graced the cover of America's most popular annual swimsuit magazine. Not to mention a tumbling swath of silky golden hair that was reputed to be insured for millions.

But what threw him, as he sat watching her share drinks with her girlfriends at a trattoria in Navigli in the southwest of Milan as dusk closed in over the city, was *his* reaction to *her*.

He was seated at a tiny round table close enough that he could hear the husky rasp of her voice as she ordered a glass of Chianti, the textured nuance of it sliding across his skin like a particularly potent aphrodisiac. Close enough that he could see her catlike, truly amazing eyes were of the deepest blue—the color of the glacially sculpted lakes of the Italian Alps that met his eyes when he opened his curtains in the morning.

Close enough to observe the self-conscious look she threw back at his stare.

And wasn't that amazing? Surely a woman of such world-renowned beauty knew the reaction she elicited in men? Surely she'd been well aware of it when she'd ensnared Giovanni and had him purchase a three-million-euro luxury apartment for her in the hopes of continuing within the style to which she'd become accustomed?

Surely she knew the combined effect of it all was somewhat like a sucker punch to the solar plexus of just about every man on this planet, which he, to his chagrin, was also not immune to.

His mouth twisted into that familiar scowl of late. Olivia Fitzgerald—the Helen of Troy of her time.

Her girlfriends, two beautiful dark-haired Italian girls, giggled and glanced his way. He pulled his gaze back to the menu, sighed and ordered a glass of wine from the *cameriera*. The private investigator who'd helped Adamo uncover who was living in the apartment in Corso Venezia had been a gold mine of information on Olivia Campbell, as she'd been calling herself. She didn't socialize much, spent most of her days holed up in her luxury abode, but she did have a faithful yoga date with her girlfriends on Thursday nights, followed by drinks at this popular spot on the canals in Navigli.

It had been a stroke of luck that the café that sat on the water of the picturesque canals was owned by an old family friend of the Mondellis… No problem obtaining a prime location to study the flaxen-haired sycophant.

He had thought of waiting until she was at the apartment to confront her, but in his current black mood, he wanted the woman who'd taken his grandfather for a ride out on the street. *Yesterday.*

He sat back and crossed one long leg over the other. Watched as the three women engaged in animated conversation. She hadn't, he observed grimly, been struck down with grief at the loss of her lover. Was she even now out hunting her next conquest before her life of luxury was unceremoniously cut off? Was that what the self-conscious looks were about?

A wave of hostility spread through him, firing his blood. He forced out a smile as the *cameriera* set his drink down in front of him, wrapped his fingers around the glass and took a long swallow. Maybe this hadn't been such a good idea, hunting Olivia Fitzgerald down when his emotions were so high. His meeting with Renzo Rialto had not gone well. The arrogant bastard was convinced Rocco was a loose cannon without a guiding force now that Giovanni was gone, and had suggested exactly what Adamo had anticipated. "Settle down, Rocco," he'd encouraged. "Show me you are ready to take on the full responsibility of Mondelli and I will give it to you."

He growled and slapped the glass back down on the table. It was going to take more than an overblown bag of wind to make him say, "I do." Hadn't the Columbia Four vowed "single forever?" Weren't women the source of every great man's downfall? Wasn't it far more rewarding to have your fill of a female when you craved it, then leave her behind when you were done?

He thought so.

In a salute to the missing three, he lifted his glass and downed a healthy gulp of the dark, plum-infused wine. His gaze moved over Olivia Fitzgerald, registering the rosy glow of attraction in her perfect, lightly tanned skin as she stole another look at him.

A plan started to form in his head. He liked it. He liked it a lot. It was perfect for his reckless, messy mood.

He was watching her. Flirting with her.

Olivia tried to smother the butterflies negotiating wide, swooping paths through her stomach, but it was impossible to remain unaffected by the Italian's stare. It was like being singed by a human torch. Hot. Focused. *On her.* And why? He was undoubtedly the most attractive man she'd ever seen in her life, and given she'd traveled the world working with beautiful men of all backgrounds, that was saying something. *She*, on the other hand, was dressed in jeans, a scrappy T-shirt with a zip-up sweatshirt over it, had no makeup on and had thrown her sweat-dampened hair into a ponytail after her yoga class—virtually unrecognizable as the top model she'd once been.

She averted her gaze from his rather petulant pout, sure women threw themselves at his feet at the slightest hint of it. For the whole package, really. But the impression he made lingered. He seemed familiar, somehow, the broad sweep of his high cheekbones framing lush, beautifully shaped lips, a square jaw and an intense dark gaze.

She frowned. Was he a model she'd worked with? Had he recognized her? But even as she thought it, she knew she would have remembered him. How would you ever forget *that* specimen of manliness? *Impossible.* His utter virility and overt confidence were of the jaw-dropping variety.

Violetta yawned, threw her hair over her shoulder and drained her wineglass. "I need to go home and study. And since *he*," she lamented, giving the gorgeous stranger a long look, "is eating *you* up, I might as well go home and pout."

"That's because Olivia is stunning." Sophia sighed. "She is blonde and exotic."

"I wish I had *your* olive skin," Olivia pointed out.

"We trade," Sophia said teasingly, reaching for her bags. "I bet the minute we leave, he's over here, Liv. And about time, too. You haven't even looked at a man since we met."

Because she'd been treasuring her stress-free escape from reality... Because she was only just now feeling like herself again...forging a new identity. Because getting close to a man had meant he might recognize her, and she didn't want to be Olivia Fitzgerald right now.

Also, because none of them had made her pulse flutter like it was at this moment.

Violetta got to her feet and threw some euros on the table. Sophia followed suit.

"You can't leave me here," Olivia protested.

"We live on the opposite side of town," Violetta countered cheerfully. "And honestly, Liv, if we don't go soon, he's going to glare the table down."

"He could be a criminal," Olivia muttered. "I'll only leave."

"A criminal who wears a twenty-five-thousand-euro Rolex," Violetta whispered in her ear. "I don't think so. Enjoy yourself, Liv. Call with the juicy details."

Olivia had no intention of offering up any details, because she wasn't staying. The only reason she was out tonight was to take her mind off Giovanni and how much she missed him. She felt completely adrift without the one person who had been her anchor in this new life, where she was truly alone. Without the mentor who had spent the past year working on her fashion line with her, teaching her. And now that the girls had lifted her spirits a bit, it was time to go.

Violetta and Sophia ambled off in the direction of the metro. Olivia fumbled in her bag for money, the meager amount in there reminding her how desperate her situation was. Her job at the café paid for her spending money, but it would never be enough to afford her own place, let alone the stunning apartment Giovanni had lent her.

Biting her lip, she dug around her change purse for coins. She would figure it out. She always did.

A shadow fell over the table. She registered the rich gleam of the handsome stranger's impeccably shone shoes on the pavement before she lifted her head to take him in.

"Ciao."

He was even better looking up close, his deep brown eyes laced with a rich amber the candlelight picked up and caressed. Big. Six foot two or three, she'd venture with her model's eye. Well built—with more hard-packed muscle than the average Italian she'd seen on the streets. *Heavenly.*

"May I sit down?" he asked in perfectly accented English, taking advantage of her apparent inability to speak.

"Actually," she muttered, "I was just on my way home."

"Surely you can stay for one more drink?" He flashed a bright, perfectly white smile that drew her attention back to his amazing lips. "I stopped to enjoy the lights and a drink and found myself staring at you instead. A far worthier pursuit, I would say."

Her chest heated, the flush that started there traveling slowly up to her cheeks. It was a line, to be sure, but the best she'd ever been handed. And somehow in her vulnerable state, because he was just *that* attractive, it was difficult to say the words she knew she should.

She forced herself. "I really should go… It's getting late."

"You really should stay," he murmured, his sultry brown eyes holding hers. "Nine o'clock is early in Italy. One drink, that's all."

Perhaps it was the way he stayed on his feet and gave her the space to say no. Or maybe it was the fact she just so very much wanted to say yes, but she found herself nodding slowly and gesturing toward the seat across from her.

"Please."

He sat, lowering his tall frame into the rather frail-looking chair. The waitress fluttered to his side the minute he crooked a finger, as if sent from above. He ordered two glasses of Chianti for them in rapid-fire Italian accompanied by one of those wide smiles, and the waitress almost fell over herself in her haste to do his bidding.

"Are you a regular here?" Olivia asked, amused, his behavior oddly relaxing, as if that type of confidence simply had to be obeyed and she might as well go with it.

"The café belongs to an old family friend of mine." The words rolled off his tongue, smooth as silk as he leaned forward and held out his hand. "Tony."

"Liv." She allowed her fingers to curl around his. The fact that he had not recognized her sent a warm current of relief through her. Or perhaps that was more a by-product of the heated, somewhat electric energy he imparted through his strong grip.

"Liv." He repeated the word as if trying it on for size and sat back, crossing his arms over his chest. "Your friends left rather suddenly. I hope I didn't chase them away."

A smile curved her lips. "You *meant* to chase them away."

He spread his hand wide. "Caught in the act. I so appreciate that about you Americans. So direct. It's refreshing."

"The New York accent is that obvious?"

"Unmistakable. I lived there for four years doing my business degree at Columbia."

The reason his English was so perfect… She gave him a long look. "If we're being direct, I'd ask you what you're doing here alone without a beautiful woman on your arm. Asking a complete stranger to have a drink with you."

His gaze darkened with a hint of something she couldn't read. He flicked a wrist toward the lights glimmering on the water. "I was looking for a little peace. Some answers to a question I had."

That intrigued her. "Did you find them?"

His mouth quirked. "Maybe."

She felt the inquisitive probe of his gaze right down to the lower layers of her dermis, the indolent way he looked at her suggesting he had all the time in the world to know her. "So what do you do, then, beautiful Liv, when you aren't sitting here?"

She couldn't help but feel like she was being led somewhere he wanted her to go, but the casually issued compliment had a much more potent effect than it should have.

"I'm a designer." She called herself that for the first time since she'd come to Milan a year ago to pursue her dream, somehow tonight needing to assert it as fact in the wake of her mentor's demise. "I'm working on my debut line."

Which hopefully would still see the light of day with Giovanni gone.

He lifted a brow. "You will partner with one of the design houses here?"

"That is the plan, yes."

"Did you study fashion in school?"

"Yes, at Pratt in New York."

His gaze turned inquisitive. "Why not stay there and start your career where you have roots?"

Because she was running from a life she never intended to return to.

"I needed a change…a fresh start."

"Milan is certainly the place to do that if you are a designer." He smiled at the waitress as she arrived with their drinks, then waited until she'd left before raising his glass. "To new…*friendships*."

Her pulse skittered across her skin like hot oil in a pan. She lifted her glass and pointed it at him. "And to you finding answers."

A slow, easy smile twisted his lips. "I think maybe meeting you was exactly what I needed."

That turned her insides completely upside down. She took a sip of her Chianti, discovered it was a significantly nicer vintage than the one she'd ordered and took some extra fortifying sips.

He crossed muscular arms over each other and sat back in the chair. "Have you had success with any of the design houses here?"

"I had made some inroads, yes, until something beyond my control happened. Now I'm not so sure it's going to work out."

"Why is that?"

She lifted her chin, fought the burn of emotion at the back of her eyes. "Life."

He was silent for a moment, then dipped his head. "I am sure you will find alternate avenues."

She nodded determinedly. "I intend to. You do what it takes, right? To make your dreams come true?"

His mouth twisted, a strange light filling his dark eyes. "You do indeed."

It was like a coldness had enveloped the warm Navigli night, the way the warmth drained from his expression. Olivia shifted in her seat, wondering when the breeze had kicked up. Wondering what she'd said or done to bring the mood change about—because everyone had dreams, didn't they? They were good things, not bad.

She took another sip of her wine. "So," she murmured in an attempt to lighten the mood, "you know what I do. Your turn to spill."

He arched a brow at her. "Spill?"

"Confess. Tell me your secrets… At least, what you do for a living."

"Aah." His mouth tilted. "I push money around. Make things profitable. Ensure the *creatives* don't bring the ship down."

She gave him a look of mock offense. "Where would the civilized world be without us?"

"True." His half smile sent a frisson of awareness through her. Made her hot all over again. She had a feeling he did that easily. Ran hot and cold. Turned it on and off like a switch.

His gaze probed hers. "What?"

"You do that easily."

"Do what easily?"

"Run hot and cold."

An amused, slightly dangerous glint filled his eyes. He set his wineglass down with a deliberate movement, his gaze on hers. "Possibly very true. Out of curiosity, Liv, which would you like me to be?"

Her heart skipped a beat. "I think I'll abstain from answering that."

"Forever or just for now?" he jibed.

"For now," she said firmly. She focused on the inch of ruby-red liquid left in her glass. She hadn't flirted with a man since the beginning of her unspectacular, long-term relationship with Guillermo Villanueva, a photographer she'd met on a job and eventually lived with. They had been finished for over a year now, and she was sorely out of practice when it came to flirting.

"Have you eaten?" He lifted an inquiring brow as she glanced up at him.

"I was going to eat when I got home."

He picked up the menu and scanned it. Ordered a selection of appetizers without consulting her. Surprisingly, for a woman who valued her independence above all else, she found it a huge turn-on. Found everything about him a huge turn-on. And it only seemed to get worse as they chatted about everything from French and American politics to books and music. He was clearly way above average intelligence, sophisticated and seemed to have vast amounts of knowledge housed under that compelling facade.

"Why Columbia?" she asked as she snared the last piece of bruschetta. "Did you have family in America?"

He shook his head. "I wanted a change of pace like you did. To spread my wings. New York as the epicenter of it all made sense."

"So are you a financial genius, then? Million-dollar deals and all that?"

A glitter entered his eyes. "The genius part is debatable, but yes, sometimes there are big deals."

She found herself staring at his mouth again. It really was lush. Spectacular. What would it be like to kiss him? What would it be like for him to kiss *her*? Oh, God. She pushed her empty wineglass away with an abrupt movement. Enough of that.

He inclined his head toward the glass. "Another?"

She shook her head. "I should get home. I have a lot I want to accomplish tomorrow."

"I'll drive you, then." He lifted his hand to signal the waitress.

She wanted to say yes. Wanted him to drive her home so he could kiss her good-night. But that was utter madness. She *didn't* know him. He *could* be a criminal. A high-end one with a Rolex and great shoes.

He looked up at their server as she took his credit card and ran it through the machine. "I would like to drive this young woman home, Cecilia. Can you offer me a reference?"

The brunette let out a husky chuckle, her gaze moving to Olivia. "He is perfectly respectable. If uncatchable."

Olivia had no doubts about that. She got to her feet, gathered her gym bag and purse and allowed Tony to guide her through the crowded little trattoria, his hand on the small of her back electrifying. They walked a short distance down a side street to where his insanely expensive-looking yellow monster of a car was parked at the curb.

He tucked her inside with a sure hand. She felt her heart rev to life as the engine rumbled beneath them, snarling like the beast it was. Pressing a palm to her throat, she gave him the directions to her apartment and tried to remember the last time she'd felt this alive. Like herself... The past year had been about finding herself again, stopping the nightmares, ending the pain.

Who was she now? She didn't even know.

Tony was quiet in the car, his elegant, eminently capable hands guiding the powerful vehicle through the streets to the aristocratic neighborhood that bounded Corso Venezia and Via Palestro, her home for the past year. Her chest pulsed with a funny ache as they passed the stunning examples of baroque and neoclassical architecture that lined the streets, the elegant exclusive avenues of Milan's fashion district. The beautiful palazzo that lay only a stone's throw from her window. Every day she sat there drinking coffee, dreaming up designs and feeding the voraciously hungry birds that knew her now. It was *hers*, this neighborhood. She'd finally found a sense of belonging and she didn't want to give it up.

Tony turned into the driveway of her modern building located in one of the neighborhoods tucked in behind Corso Venezia. When Giovanni had shown it to her, she'd instantly fallen in love with its wrought iron balconies and wall-size liberty windows. With its feeling of lightness after the prison New York had become...

Tony brought the car to a halt in the rounded driveway. "Do you have a parking spot? I'll see you to your door."

Her already agitated heartbeat sped up. She knew exactly where this was leading if he accompanied her up to her apartment, and for a woman who had never done this, never invited a man back to her apartment on a first date, it was like someone had dropped her onto one of those death-defying loop-the-loop roller coasters that promised equal amounts of terror and exhilaration.

She shook her head, dry mouthed, realizing he was waiting for a response. "It's underground," she told him huskily, pointing to the entrance at the end of the driveway.

He guided the car into the garage, parked in her spot and followed her to the elevators. They rode the glass-enclosed lift up to her tenth-floor apartment.

"An awfully exclusive apartment for a struggling artist," Tony commented, leaning back against the wall.

Olivia pressed damp palms against her thighs as the cityscape came into view. "A friend was helping me out."

His brow rose. "A *friend*?"

"A *nonromantic* friend," she underscored, absorbing the aggressive, predatory male in him. It wasn't helping the state of her insides.

His raised brows arced into a slashing V. "Men just don't *lend* multimillion-euro apartments to a female unless they have other intentions, Liv."

The insinuation in his words brought her chin up. "This one did," she rasped. The elevator doors swung open. She stalked out of the car and headed down the hallway to her apartment, her head a muddled, attracted mess.

Tony caught up with her at her door. She turned to face him, confused, her stomach a slow burn. "I think you don't know me at all."

"My mistake," he came back laconically, tall and daunting. "It's a natural question for a man to ask."

Was it? They'd only had a drink. She was so confused about the whole evening, about what was happening with this beautiful stranger, her head spun. She stood there, heart hammering in her chest. Tony put a hand to the wall beside her, keeping a good six or seven inches between them, his gaze pinned on her face. Her stomach dropped as if she was headed toward the steepest plunge on that scary roller coaster, the part where one had big, huge second thoughts.

Something glimmered in his gaze. "Aren't you going to invite me in for an espresso to cap the evening off?"

"I don't know," she answered honestly, knees weak.

"Oh, come on, Liv," he chided, that glimmer darkening into a challenge. "Men are territorial. Would you expect a man like me not to be?"

No. Yes. Her head swam.

He closed the gap between them until he was mere inches from her. His palm came up to cup her jaw, his gaze dropping to her lips. Her own clung shamelessly to that lush pout she'd been staring at all night, had been wanting to kiss all night. And he knew it.

He lowered his head and rocked his mouth over hers. Smooth, questing, he exerted just the right amount of pressure not to frighten her away, and that mouth, *that mouth*, was sensational. She anchored her palms against the solid planes of his chest, her bones sinking into the hard line of the wall as he explored the curves of her mouth. He kissed her so expertly she never had a chance. All she could do was helplessly follow his lead. When he delved deeper, demanded entrance to the heat of her mouth, she opened for him.

Their tongues slid along each other's in an erotic duel that rendered her knees useless. She dug her fingertips harder into his chest, breathing him in, registering how delicious he smelled. He was a potent combination of heady male and tangy lime, and she was completely and irrevocably lost.

He pulled back, his gaze scouring her face. "Your key," he prompted harshly.

Her brain struggled to process the command. Blood pumping, head full, she rummaged through her purse, found her keys and handed them to him.

The sane part of Rocco told him he didn't need to carry the charade any further. It was obvious Olivia Fitzgerald was not above falling into the arms of a man with a beautiful watch and a nice car if it meant rescuing her from her precarious position. Whether she displayed an irresistible vulnerability along with it was inconsequential. It was likely a well-rehearsed act.

The less-than-rational part of his brain wanted to see how far she'd let him take it. How desperate she was.

He tossed her keys on the entryway table. Watched her sink her small white teeth into her perfectly shaped bottom lip.

"I'm not so interested in coffee," he admitted harshly, watching her pupils dilate. "Do you mind if we skip it?"

She shook her head, eyes wide. Worried her lip with

those perfect teeth. He closed the distance between them, the heat they created together rising up to tighten his chest. He swallowed hard at the swift kick of lust that rocketed through him as he brought his palms to rest on either side of her where she stood, back against the door. It was inconceivable to him that he could feel such desire for her given who she was, what she had been to his grandfather, even if this was a deliberate experiment to extract the truth. But she was undeniably exquisite.

Her cheeks, tanned to a light golden brown from the hot Milanese summer sun, were flushed with desire. Her chest under the worn purple T-shirt was rising and falling fast, her nipples erect against the soft fabric. Her hands lay limp at her sides, as if she had no idea what to do with them.

He did. He wanted them on him, sliding over every inch of his hot skin until he rolled her under him and made her his. *Dio.* This was insanity.

He dipped his hands under the frayed edge of her T-shirt and sought out the silky-soft bare skin beneath. She was enough to tempt a levelheaded man to mad acts, even his rigidly correct grandfather who had never looked at another woman after his Rosa had died. Her swift intake of breath echoed in the silent apartment as he trailed his fingers over the bare skin of her flat stomach, her midriff, the muscles of her abdomen tensing beneath his touch. Her head dropped back against the door, eyes almost purple as she waited for his kiss.

"You could bring the strongest man to his knees," he muttered roughly, almost angrily, as he brought his mouth down to hers. "But then you know that, don't you, Liv?"

Her brows came together in a frown, her lips parting to answer him. He didn't let her get that far, his mouth taking hers in an insistent kiss that allowed no hesitation. She was rigid under his hands for a moment, as if teetering in indecision. He took her tongue inside his mouth, drawing her back into the heat. She was soft and perfect and he could not resist the lure of her flesh, bare beneath the T-shirt.

He pushed her jacket off her shoulders, letting it drop to the floor. "Lift your arms."

She did, her gaze on his as he pulled the threadbare T-shirt over her head, tossed it to the floor and drank her in. She was slim, perfect, with high, firm breasts and rose-colored nipples that were tautly aroused.

It was like being in the Garden of Eden and told not to touch. He just couldn't do it.

Bending his head, he palmed her breast, taking the rosy tip into his mouth. Her swift intake of breath made his blood heat. He sucked on her, laved her, until she was moaning, moving restlessly against him, then he transferred his attention to the other rounded peak. The feel, the taste of her underneath his mouth, was like forbidden fruit. *Irresistible.* The sound of their connection filled the hot Milanese night, breathy, seeking. He slid his thigh between hers and filled his hands with the rounded, toned curves of her bottom, seeking relief for his aching flesh.

Her gasp filled his ear. *"Tony."*

One word, one softly uttered admission of surrender, was all it took to bring him crashing back to earth. To know he had proved what he had come here to do.

He lifted his head, sank his hands into her waist and pushed her away.

"The name is Rocco."

Her eyes widened, darkened. A frown furrowed her brow as her hands came up to cover herself. "Rocco? Why did you tell me your…" Her voice trailed off as the color drained from her face.

"That's right, Liv," he said harshly, taking great pleasure in her look of horror. "Antonio is my middle name. How does it feel to sink your hooks into two generations of Mondellis?"

Her look of complete confusion was award worthy. She shook her head, gaze fixed on his. "What are you talking about? Giovanni and I were not like that."

"What were you, then?" His tone was savage. "You expect me to believe a man buys you a three-million-euro luxury apartment out of the goodness of his heart? Because you're *friends*? My grandfather has not talked about you *once*, has never even mentioned you in passing conversation. And yet you were *together*?"

"Because I didn't want anyone to know I was here." She snatched her T-shirt up from the floor and pulled it over her head. "Giovanni was protecting my privacy. He was my mentor. My *friend*. He was not my lover. How could you even think that? It's preposterous."

Fury lanced through him. He stepped forward until they were nose to nose. "No more than a seventy-year-old man thinking *you* could be interested in him." He waved a hand at her. "You must be good, I'll hand you that. What man could resist you servicing him? Moaning his name as if you can't wait to get into bed?"

She was in front of him so fast, her palm arcing through the air, she almost got it to his face before he snatched it away and yanked it down to her side.

"You bastard," she snarled at him, her catlike eyes spitting fire as he held her hand captive. "How *dare* you make accusations about something you know nothing about?"

"Because I *know* him," he raged. "Giovanni was hopelessly, irrevocably in love with my grandmother. There is no way he would take a twentysomething lover unless he was completely *taken in. Brainwashed with lust.*"

She glared at him. "He didn't. I keep trying to tell you that."

He kept his fingers manacled around her wrist as she tried to tug her hand free. "Why are you hiding out from the world here? Why not use your name to build your line, if that was the truth—if that is your dream?"

"It *was* the truth." She wrenched her arm free, her show of strength taking him off guard. "Everything I said tonight was the truth. I needed to get away from modeling, from *everything*, so I came here."

"To escape your creditors?"

"To escape *my life*." She pointed to the door. "Get the hell out of my apartment. *Now*."

"*My* apartment, you mean." He gave her a searching look. "Why Giovanni, Olivia? Why choose a seventy-year-old man as your lover when you could have anyone? Any rich man on this planet would welcome you into his bed. Pleasure you with the youth of a much younger man. All you would have to do is snap your fingers."

Her hands curled into fists by her sides. "You are so unbelievably wrong."

"Then why the checks? Why was Giovanni doling out cash to you on a regular basis? Was that also *friendship*?"

Her mouth flattened into a defiant line. She closed her eyes, a long silence stretching between them. When she opened them, her eyes glimmered with a wealth of emotion he couldn't read.

"We were building a line together. The money was for fabrics. For suppliers."

He gave her an incredulous look. "I am the CEO of House of Mondelli, Olivia. I know every project Giovanni was working on because he was a creative and he tended to go off half-cocked with new ideas without exploring their viability. There was no line."

She stalked around him and headed down the hallway. He followed her into the bright, large room at the back of the apartment. Dozens of designs hung from a rack along the back wall. A sewing machine sat on a table. Stacks of illustrations lay scattered across a table.

He walked over and fingered some of the designs. They were beautiful, ethereal creations that even the noncreative in him could see were sensational, different, stamped with a unique sense of freedom of fabric and color that was distinct from anything he'd seen before. But they also featured a Giovanni-like sense of symmetry.

An odd emotion stirred to life inside of him. Riled him. "This doesn't prove anything. All it proves is that you were using my grandfather to further your ambition. What did you say in the café? You do what it takes to make your dreams come true?"

Some of her newly found color drained from her face. "You're taking that way out of context."

"I think I've got it just right. You have a drink with a complete stranger, a man with an expensive watch who clearly does well, you see your opportunity for another rich benefactor and you make your move." He tossed his head in disgust. "I could have had you against that door. You were ready to replace Giovanni *seven days after his death*."

Her pallor took on a grayish tinge. "You set that all up tonight to see if I was a gold digger?"

"And wasn't it telling?" He gave her a mirthless, half smile. "The idea actually didn't come into my head until I sat there watching you and your *fidanzate* laughing and giggling as if your lover hadn't just passed away. I wanted to see what kind of a woman you were before I tossed your beautiful little behind out on the street and now I know."

Her head reared back. "I was out tonight to try to take my mind off Giovanni. I can't expect to understand how much you must be grieving him. I know you were close. But *I* am grieving him, too. I cared for him. And I will not permit you to sully what we had with your wild accusations."

"It's the truth," he gritted.

"It's far from it."

"Then spit it out. I am craving a little honesty here."

She took a deep breath. Pushed stray strands of hair that had escaped her ponytail out of her face. "Your grandfather was in love with two women. Madly, fully in love with two people. One of those women was my mother, Tatum."

He stared at her. "What the hell are you talking about?"

She sucked her bottom lip between her teeth. "When my mother modeled for Mondelli in the eighties, she had an affair with Giovanni. Giovanni was torn between her and Rosa, agonized over the decision, he said. In the end, he chose Rosa and severed all ties with my mother. Rosa knew about the affair, but neither she nor Giovanni spoke of it afterward."

He gave her a look of disbelief. Giovanni in love with Tatum Fitzgerald? While he'd been married to his grandmother? He may not have much of a belief in the concept of true love, but the one person he'd seen have it was his grandfather with Rosa. They'd conceived Sandro when his grandmother was just eighteen, had been each other's first loves and had remained deeply enamored until Rosa had passed away.

An affair? It was inconceivable.

He leveled a gaze at her. "How do you know all this?"

A nerve pulsed in her cheek. "I was going through a rough time in my modeling career. Giovanni approached me at an industry function in New York. I think he felt guilty about what happened to my mother's career after he ended things. She fell apart after he left her. She went on to marry my father, but she never got over Giovanni and they divorced. Giovanni told me the whole story that night."

He attempted to absorb the far-fetched tale. "So he decided to *befriend* you? Put you up in a luxury apartment in Milan and mentor you because he felt guilty over a relationship that ended *decades* ago?"

She lifted her chin. "He knew I needed a friend. Someone I could count on. He was there for me."

"What about your own family and friends?"

"They aren't something I can turn to." Her gaze dropped away from his. "I left my whole life behind when I came to Milan."

Because she'd known she had a free ride. He smothered a frustrated growl and paced to the window. "So Giovanni is just your friend, you were out tonight missing him, and that thing with me just now was what? The way you treat all men who chat you up in a café?"

"You *deliberately* tried to seduce me."

He swung around. "And *how* seducible you were, *bella*. You made it easy."

Her expression hardened. "If you choose not to believe a word I say, you can leave. I'll be out within the week."

"Tell me the truth about you and Giovanni and I'll give you a month. I'm not an unreasonable man."

Her eyes flashed. "Get out."

He thought that might be a good idea before he lost what was left of his head. Putting his hands on Olivia Fitzgerald, *coming here*, had been a mistake driven by his grief and his desire to know what had been in Giovanni's head these past months. And now it was time to rectify it by getting the hell out.

He swept his gaze over the racks of clothes. She was going to have an issue finding a place she could afford that could accommodate all of *this* without Giovanni bankrolling it. And even he wasn't without a heart.

"I'll give you a month. Then I expect the keys delivered to me."

She followed him to the door, looking every bit the angelic blonde damsel in distress that she was not. He walked through the door and didn't look back.

Giovanni had always been a bit of a romantic. Good thing Rocco was nothing like him.

CHAPTER THREE

ROCCO STOOD ON the tarmac of Milan's Linate Airport, Christian Markos at his side. The last of the Columbia Four to depart following Giovanni's funeral, Christian was headed to Hong Kong and a deal that couldn't wait. As always, when Rocco parted from his closest friends, there was an empty feeling in his heart. They had become so tight during those four years at Columbia. Watched one another grow into manhood and cemented their friendships as they took on the world.

Together they were an impenetrable force, greater than the sum of their parts. It was always difficult to return to their respective corners of the world, but they did so with the knowledge they would see one another soon—their four-times-a-year meet-ups a ritual none of them missed.

Christian wrapped an arm around him. "I may have a weekend off midmonth. Why don't we take your boat out? Catch up properly?"

Rocco smiled. "I'll believe it when we're drinking Peroni on the deck, *fratello*. Some big deal will come up and you'll be gone again."

Christian gave him an indignant look. "That last one was a megamerger. Out of my hands."

"And the brunette that came along with it?"

"Opposing pain in my behind," Christian grumbled. "Who was the blonde today by the way? Looked like a heated conversation."

It had been. Olivia Fitzgerald showing up at his grand-father's funeral had been an event he hadn't anticipated. Despite his objections, she'd insisted on staying. Not something he'd been willing to risk a scene over, particularly when his father had just made his own notable appearance, reeking of alcohol.

He looked at Christian. "Olivia Fitzgerald. She was not invited. I had an issue with it."

His friend lifted a brow. "Olivia Fitzgerald the model? I thought she was in hiding."

"She is, here in Milan. She knew Giovanni and wanted to pay her respects."

Christian looked curious. "What is your issue with her?"

"It's complicated."

"Everything is complicated with you." His friend shrugged. "You should sign her. The board would be kissing your feet."

"She doesn't want to be in the limelight." Why, he still didn't know.

An amused smile twisted the Greek's lips. "One of my senior deal makers had that photo of her nude on the beach in his office. I had to make him take it down. It's a little distracting when you're trying to crunch numbers."

"No doubt." Rocco knew exactly the shot his friend was talking about. The beach scene of Olivia kneeling in the surf, hands strategically covering herself, had graced the cover of an annual swimsuit magazine, then made the rounds as a wildly popular screensaver.

The engines of Christian's jet started to whir. "I'm so sorry about Giovanni," he said to Rocco. "I know how much he meant to you. And I'm sorry you had to deal with your father today. That can't have been easy."

"It was inevitable." The fact that Christian and Zayed

had had to remove his father from the proceedings—not so much.

He frowned. "I'm sorry you had to bear witness to that."

"It's not your cross to bear," his friend said quietly. "You take the weight of the world on your shoulders sometimes, Rocco. There's only so much of a burden a man can carry."

Rocco nodded. Except he'd been carrying the burden of his family for so long he didn't know how it could be any different.

"Go," he told Christian, clapping him on the back. "My boat and a case of Peroni are waiting when you come back."

His friend nodded and strode toward the plane. Rocco watched while he boarded the jet, the crew closed up the doors and the pilot taxied off to join the lineup of planes waiting to take off.

Even with everything he had on his plate, he couldn't get that night with Olivia out of his head. What she'd told him about Giovanni. Whether there was the slightest bit of truth in any of it. It sat in his brain and festered. Added to his confusion over his grandfather's decisions, the changes he'd seen in Giovanni of late. Had he been capable of cheating on his beloved Rosa? Sure, Giovanni had admired women for the pure aesthetic of them. He was a designer. But *unfaithful*?

He'd thought it had just been age softening his grandfather lately, the mellowing of his acerbic, grandiose personality. Had it instead been the influence of a woman? Olivia Fitzgerald?

Had he been in love with her? Did Olivia possess many of the same attributes as her mother, thus replacing the one woman he'd never been able to have? His stomach rearranged itself with a strange emotion he didn't want to identify. After witnessing the genius Giovanni and Olivia had created together in those designs, it was clear they had a connection.

And why did he care? What was it to him if his grandfather had fallen for a woman a third of his age? If he'd allowed himself to be made a fool of? *He* had done his job ensuring Olivia Fitzgerald would no longer take advantage of his family.

Because you almost lost your head. Over a beautiful blonde who'd had more of a master plan in *her* head than he'd ever had.

An image of Olivia's face when she'd walked into the church today flicked through his head. Fear she would be discovered even though she'd had a scarf over her head. Fear of *him* as she'd seen him. Stubborn defiance blazing in those amazing blue eyes as she'd stood her ground.

She'd also, he conceded, looked heartsick. Sad. And in his gut, he knew it was true emotion. He hadn't had the heart to toss her out. She had left as quickly as she'd appeared, not staying for the reception. He knew she was still in the apartment; he'd had the building supervisor keep him advised of her presence. He suspected she was having difficulty finding another place, but it wasn't his problem she'd lost her paycheck in Giovanni.

Christian's jet disappeared into the clouds. Rocco turned and headed toward the terminal, but his friend's words followed him. *You should sign her. The board would be kissing your feet...*

They *would* kiss his feet if he signed Olivia Fitzgerald. The worldwide press had been in a furor ever since her disappearance from modeling. She'd left on top, one of the most highly paid faces in the world. Everyone wanted her. Her disappearance had only added to the mystique.

He pushed his way through the terminal doors, strode through the tiny building and exited into the car park. There was only one problem with Christian's rather brilliant plan. Olivia didn't want to be found. Had wanted to escape her former life. And if it wasn't because she'd been bankrupt, as he'd suggested, then why? Why abandon a three-million-dollar contract when she could have just worked her way out of it, then gone into the career she'd desired?

She'd looked so miserable, so dejected, as she'd left the church today. She had no hope of launching that line without Giovanni. Her dream was done. Unless she found herself another benefactor.

He paused, his hand on the handle of the Aventador's door. Suddenly the path forward became clear. He had what Olivia needed as head of one of the most powerful design houses in the world. Olivia had what he needed if he could persuade her to come back to modeling for a year as the exclusive face of Mondelli. Her star power would turn Mondelli into a superstar brand, the couture house of the moment, the board would fall to its knees at such an acquisition and he would have control of his company again.

Adrenaline fueled his movements as he stepped into his car and brought it purring to life. Making Olivia an offer she couldn't refuse was an undeniably alluring play. But there was something else his mind was manufacturing that would be the icing on the cake. The pièce de résistance. Olivia Fitzgerald as the face of Mondelli and the brand-new fiancée of the CEO of House of Mondelli. A perfect union from all angles. And the perfect way to convince the board he had House of Mondelli as his top priority.

All his problems solved in one tidy little package.

A smile curved his mouth. Renzo Rialto would wet himself. How much more could he want? Now all he had to do was persuade Olivia Fitzgerald his plan was in both their interests.

Olivia was packing a box of design materials when the knocking sounded hard and insistent on her front door. Thinking it might be Violetta coming to help, and frowning at her exuberance, she got to her feet, dusted off her hands and went to answer it. Any distraction to take her mind off her rather desperate situation was welcome at this point.

When she saw who was standing in the hallway, she amended that thought. Any distraction *other* than a fully resplendent Rocco Mondelli clad in the dark suit he'd worn to the funeral that morning. Despite her vow to hate him, her heart pitter-pattered in her chest as she took him in leaning against the doorjamb, impatience written across his olive-skinned face.

"You said I had a month."

"You do." He walked past her into the apartment. "You'll find I'm a man of my word, Olivia. Have you had any luck yet finding another apartment?"

A man of his word? He'd deliberately seduced and misled her in this very apartment. She gave him a cool look and shut the door. "As a matter of fact, no, but I thought I'd better start getting packed up before you send in the goons."

"I won't have to." He waved a hand toward the kitchen. "This time I would like an espresso."

She stared at him in amazement. "You were ready to toss me out of that funeral this morning and now I'm supposed to make you coffee?"

He returned her stare, nonplussed. "I have an offer I think you'd like to hear."

Not in this decade.

His mouth curved. "Get me that coffee, Olivia."

Deciding she wasn't really in a position to argue because he *could* toss her out on her butt at this very moment, she walked past him to the kitchen, emptied the grinds from the espresso machine and did his bidding. He stood there, hands in his pockets, watching her.

"You were genuinely sad this morning."

She pressed the start button, turned and leaned back against the counter. "I loved Giovanni. Of course I was."

"So now it's love," he jibed. "Giovanni was madly in love with a woman and I hadn't a clue. How remarkable."

"You can walk right back out that door if this is the way this is going to go."

"*Nessuno*, Liv, it isn't." He crossed his arms over his chest and leaned back against the countertop. "I'm going to make you an offer that makes a whole lot of sense, you're going to take it and we're going to make the most of this difficult situation."

"There's nothing you could say that would convince me to have anything to do with you after what you did to me."

"I think you're wrong." He waved his hand toward the living room and the packed boxes littering every open space. "You are never going to be able to afford an apartment in Milan that will allow you to do your design work on a barista's salary. You've made it clear returning to your former life is not an option and you cannot rely on family and friends for help. So all you have left," he concluded, touching his chest, "is *me*."

"I don't want anything from you," she said pointedly, shoulders rising to her ears. "I will figure out a way."

His gaze darkened to a forbidding ebony. "What if I said I would honor the commitment Giovanni made to you? But I would take it even further. I would move the development of your line in-house at Mondelli, offer you all the design and marketing support we have and bring it to market for the fall of next year."

Her mouth dropped open. He would take the development of her line *in-house*? *Why*, when he clearly thought so little of her?

"Because you have something I want, Olivia." He answered her unspoken question with a twist of his lips. "I need a face to carry the House of Mondelli through the next year. Bridget Thomas's contract is up and I don't care to renew it. I would offer you a five-million-dollar contract for the year. You coming back to modeling would generate a great deal of excitement for the brand, make people stand up and pay attention again."

Her heart dropped. "I'm not modeling anymore. That part of my life is over."

He nodded. "I understand you want to design, that that's where your heart is. But surely one year, *twelve months of your life*, to secure your dream isn't such a hardship."

"No." The word flew out of her mouth, harsh, vehement. "I will never model again."

He pinned his gaze on her. "Why? What happened to make you give it all up?"

Her last appearance on a runway. Her best friend overdosing after walking that same runway months before… The memory of it slammed through her head, dark and terrifying. She reached back and gripped the counter, her fingertips pressing into the cold granite. She had completely lost it that night, her pressure-packed life finally eating her alive. And she was never going back.

She lifted her gaze to his. "It doesn't matter why. I left and I'm not going back."

"When the alternative is letting your dream die?" He stared at her, an incredulous look on his face. "If you debut a line with House of Mondelli you will *instantly* become a star of the design world. You won't have to build a reputation, you will have one immediately. And from there, all you need to do is choose your path. You would never have to set foot on a runway again after the twelve months."

She sank her palms into her temples and turned away. It was tempting, so tempting, to say yes. What he was saying was true. She'd thanked her lucky stars when Giovanni had taken her under his wing, because with his help she could succeed in a cutthroat industry that was almost impossible to break into. She could change her life and finally be happy. But return to modeling to make it happen? Acid inched its way up her throat. Not doable.

It would be the end of her this time.

She turned back to him, her features schooled into an expressionless mask. "I'm sorry. It's just not possible."

The incredulity on his face deepened. "I would wipe out the three-million-dollar debt you owe Le Ciel for the contract you broke."

She pulled in a deep breath. *Lord*, he was hitting all her weak spots. She would love to erase that blight on her track record. It would put her at peace with the world. But she couldn't do it. "No."

He lifted his shoulders, his gaze cool and calculating. "Then you'd better keep packing."

Desperation surged through her. "You saw the designs. They're amazing. Let me show them to you properly and you'll see how perfect they are for Mondelli's fall line. Let me bring them to market with you as Giovanni intended. The cachet of having my name attached to them, *Giovanni's* name, will give you that buzz you are looking for. It doesn't have to be me modeling."

He shook his head. "You have no cachet as a designer. I want you as the face of Mondelli. That is the only deal on the table."

"Then, no." She would rather beg on the street than go back to modeling.

"I would take some time to think about it," he advised, pushing away from the counter. "I won't ask again. And while you're at it, you might want to consider the other half of my offer."

She was almost afraid to ask what it was.

"I want to create huge buzz around our partnership. Therefore, if you accept my offer to be the face of Mondelli, we would also announce our engagement to the world at the same time. The marriage of two great brands."

Her mouth fell open, a dizzy feeling sweeping through her. *He was joking.* He had to be joking, except there wasn't one bit of humor on his beautiful face.

"That idea is preposterous."

"It's genius. A master publicity stunt."

She shook her head. "We hate each other. How would we possibly convince the world we are in love?"

A cynical smile twisted his lips. "Chemistry, Liv. We may hate each other, but neither of us would be being honest if we didn't admit that was one hell of a kiss against that door, *bella*."

"And this engagement…" she ventured weakly. "Would it be real or pretend?"

"Real?" His gaze moved scathingly over her. "You think I would take the gold digger who used my grandfather for his money as a fiancée in the true sense of the word?"

Fury singed her veins, fisting her hands at her sides. "For the last time, I didn't use him."

"It doesn't matter." He waved a hand at her. "All of that is inconsequential now. I'm offering you a way out of your situation. Our engagement would cover the period of your contract with Mondelli. Once you've fulfilled it, we go our separate ways—*uncouple*, as it's fashionably put these days. You will have your line with Mondelli and my promise to support you every step of the way."

This time she *was* speechless. He wanted her to act as his fiancée? She'd had to acquire the skills of an actress to model, but this was way, *way* beyond her skill set.

"Absolutely not," she said firmly. "I will never return to modeling. If that's the only form your proposal will take, I'll have to decline."

He shrugged. "It's your decision. You have a week to come to me. After that the offer is off the table, this apartment is no longer yours and you, Olivia, better have a backup plan."

She watched as he turned on his heel and left, apparently not that interested in the espresso this time around, either. The sound of the door thudding shut made her wince. She had no backup plan. She had no plan at all. All she had was a beautiful apartment she desperately didn't want to leave, a life she'd built here she loved and an almost complete fall line that would make all her dreams come true if the House of Mondelli put its name behind it.

Everywhere she looked, she was out of options. Out of time. And that bastard knew it. He damn well knew it.

CHAPTER FOUR

OLIVIA SPENT THE rest of the week scouring Milan for apartments that would accommodate her work. She grew more dismayed with each visit. None of them were big enough, even if she did take on a roommate to afford one. The luxury apartment Giovanni had given her use of was palatial in comparison.

The end of her shift at the café at hand, she pulled her apron over her head, drew herself an espresso from the machine and sat down at one of the tables outside. She had to be out of the apartment tomorrow. The only thing she could do was pack up her designs, move into Violetta's already overcrowded house and pound doors to see if a local designer would take her on—which was unlikely, given how ultracompetitive the marketplace was.

Or she could go home, tail between her legs, and try to work some of her New York contacts. But New York wasn't going to be an easier nut to crack, and the thought of answering the inevitable questions when doors did open made her stomach knot. She wasn't ready to go back.

Panic rose up inside of her, her fingers curling tight around the handle of her cup. If she'd been more on top of her career, her finances, she wouldn't be in this situation. She never would have let her mother take control and fritter the money away. A *lot* of money. But preoccupied with pressure-packed million-dollar assignments and endorsements, traveling out of a suitcase more often than not, barely knowing what time zone she was in, let alone keeping her head above water, she'd had put her trust in the one person she'd thought she could.

Her mother had never been able to hold a real job when her career had fizzled out, and Olivia's father, Deacon Fitzgerald, had left when she was eight. A B-list photographer, her father had abandoned his career and started over with a new family and a new job at the transit company in a bid to erase the woman who had broken his heart. Olivia and her mother had sputtered along with whatever money her father could provide and her mother's spotty, on-again, off-again jobs until Olivia's career had taken off and Tatum had put the only skills she had, managing *her*, to work making her daughter a household name. But the more money Olivia had made, the faster it had gone, and the vicious, never-ending cycle was cemented.

The discovery she was broke on the heels of her best friend Petra Danes's overdose had sent her on a tailspin she'd never recovered from. The money had been her way out, and when that door was closed she'd quite literally self-destructed that last night in New York.

She took a sip of the coffee, the acrid brew harsh on her tongue. She'd come to Milan because she couldn't do it anymore. She was not healed; she needed time. That hadn't changed.

She watched as one exquisitely dressed Italian after another strolled by, the women in designer dresses even for a trip to the market. Turning to her father in her darkest time, for emotional support if not financial, hadn't been an option. She'd been so young when he'd left she'd hardly known him. And though they'd met regularly for a while until she was a teenager, each time she'd seen him it had grown more awkward and painful, as if her father had wanted to put as much distance between him and his old life as he could. So Olivia had stopped trying to see him, and he'd stopped calling except on big occasions like her birthday. And that was the way it had been ever since.

She bit her lip, refusing to get emotional over a parent lottery she'd lost a long time ago. A resigned clarity fell over her. She had only two choices: give up or accept Rocco Mondelli's offer. And since giving up her dream wasn't on the table, it left her only with the option to return to a career she'd vowed she never would. To an industry that had almost eaten her alive.

Her lashes fluttered down. Something Giovanni had said to her in those early dark days filled her head. *Passion is what makes life worth living,* ragazza mia. *If you don't have it in your soul, it dies a day at a time. Stop thinking of what you must do and start thinking of what will save you.*

And that was how she finally made her decision.

Olivia Fitzgerald showed up at his office forty-eight hours after Rocco had predicted she would. He instructed his assistant, Gabriella, to show her in. Gabriella appeared seconds later with Olivia at her side, an expectant look on his assistant's face.

"Go home," he instructed his PA. "I'm on my way out, as well. *Buona serata.*"

Gabriella echoed his farewell and disappeared. Olivia stood just inside the doorway, her carefully controlled expression veiling whatever thoughts were going on in her beautiful head. The tap of her toe on the marble was the only indicator she was apprehensive about what she'd come to do, and he liked that there was at least one outward sign filling him in on the inside picture.

The outside view was undeniably compelling. Her dark jeans made the most of her long legs, the cut of her clingy jersey shirt emphasizing her cool blonde beauty. Her hair was caught up in a ponytail once again, big dark sunglasses perched on her head as if to say she wasn't coming out of hiding until absolutely forced to.

He felt his nerve receptors react to her with that same layers-deep effect she'd had on him that night in Navigli. Even without makeup, she was still the most arresting woman he'd ever laid eyes on.

She lifted her chin as he brought his gaze slowly back up to her face. "If you're on your way out, we can do this another time."

"I'm on my way home." He got to his feet and reached for his briefcase. "I'm staying at my apartment in Milan tonight. We can talk there."

"This won't take long," she supplied hastily. "No need for that."

His mouth twisted. "I'm assuming you've come to take me up on my offer?"

Her lips pressed together. "Yes."

"Then we have lots to talk about. We can do it over dinner." He tossed the file he'd been working on into his briefcase, along with another pile of documents.

"I don't want to intrude on your evening. Why don't we…"

"Olivia." He lifted his head and pinned his gaze on hers. "Let's get something straight right off the top. In this relationship, I talk and you listen. I make the rules. You follow them. In no way is this going to be an equal, democratic partnership. Not for the money I'm paying you."

Her mouth dropped open. "I haven't signed your deal yet."

"But you will, because you're here." He dropped a last sheaf of papers in the briefcase and snapped it shut.

She sank her hands into her hips, her sapphire eyes a vivid blue beam blazing into him. "That night in Navigli must have been an aberration. Is *this* how you really treat your women? Favor them with a wild night in bed so they'll nip at your heels as required?"

He smiled at that. "Usually I have a bit more finesse, but in this case, it isn't necessary. Make no mistake about it, Olivia, Navigli was about me finding out what kind of a woman you really are. That was all."

Better she chew on that than the naked, unadulterated urge he felt to show her that wild ride in bed before he brought her to heel. Because this was a business arrangement. She had been Giovanni's lover. And rule number one for this particular business arrangement was to keep his hands off his soon-to-be pretend fiancée.

She flashed him a defiant look. "Helpful, then, for our little charade that you are such a magnificent actor. You fooled me with that kiss. It almost felt as if you meant it."

He lifted a brow, his gaze raking over her face. "As much as I'm loath to damage your ego heading into this very important assignment for both of us, I'm afraid my taste runs to sophisticated brunettes of a European bent. So you are quite safe, *cara*, from me."

She flinched, a tiny, almost indiscernible retraction he would have missed had he not been studying her so intently. *Bene.* The more they ignored the undeniable attraction between them, the better.

Her long, gold-tipped lashes came down to veil her eyes. "Too bad you're saddled with a very blonde, outspoken American fiancée for a year."

He gave her a slow smile. "I can handle you, Olivia, and you know it."

"You *think* you can because you are the epitome of arrogance." Fire lit the blue gaze she trained on him. "How is this going to work, then? Your overactive libido is well documented. Do we act as a joyous engaged couple while you engage in a discreet liaison or two on the side?"

He shifted his weight to both feet, widening his stance,

his laconic smile intensifying. "Who said I have an over-active libido? I would call it standard for a young, healthy male."

She lifted a shoulder. "Your reputation speaks for itself." Her gaze rested on him assessingly. "Giovanni thought it reflected a certain…emotional immaturity on your part. That you use it to avoid attachment."

"Emotional immaturity?" His head jerked back. "He said that?"

She nodded. "He thought you and Alessandra suffered from not having a direct parental influence while growing up. He said he did the best he could, but it's not the same as having your own parents to guide you."

He stared speechlessly at her, absorbing the look of satisfaction on her face. He'd started this war of words, yes. But *her* telling him his grandfather's innermost thoughts, thoughts that had apparently played a part in his decision to give Rocco a mere 50 percent stake in House of Mondelli? His fists itched to find the nearest wall and bury themselves in it. Giovanni had trusted his *twenty-six-year-old lover* enough to confide his thoughts in her, but not him?

He worked his jaw. Gathered his composure before he said something else to tip his cards. "What other confidences did Giovanni elect to illuminate you with?"

She gave him a wary look, as if realizing she might have gone too far. "He only made the odd comment here and there when we were talking about family. He was a private man, Rocco."

Apparently not that private. He jammed his hands in his pockets and impaled her with his gaze. "To answer your question, there will be no liaisons for either of us. This is a five-million-dollar partnership, Olivia, plus what I had to pay Le Ciel to break the contract you reneged on. We don't mess it up because we have to satisfy an urge. I can do that in the shower."

Her cheeks flamed a rosy pink. "That discussion was more for your benefit than mine. I'm just trying to understand the ground rules."

He picked up his briefcase and jacket. "They will become eminently clear as we discuss them over dinner. Shall we?"

She was silent as he drove them the short distance to the Mondelli penthouse, and he was glad for it, still steaming over the inside track she seemed to have on Giovanni's thoughts.

His frustration had abated, somewhat, by the time they reached the Galleria Passarella area in the heart of Milan. He should be *estatico*. He had exactly what he wanted after all. The perfect jewel to dangle in front of the board to cement his control of the company he'd helped build. He was no longer sporting the shorter end of the stick in this power struggle, and it felt good. More than good.

The penthouse occupied the top three floors of a graceful, modern building with superb views of the city. Rocco had chosen it because of the uniqueness of its design, the hidden jewel it contained. With the living quarters located on the ninth floor, the architect had used the tenth and eleventh floors to create a garden paradise that overlooked the city, including a terrace big enough to entertain fifty and a rock-pool retreat.

They stopped on the ninth floor, where he requested a light meal for him and Olivia from his housekeeper, then he led the way up the stone staircase to the roof garden. He could tell from the wide-eyed wonder in her eyes Olivia loved it instantly.

"It's hard to imagine this could exist up here."

"Exactly why I bought it. The heaters I had built in keep it the perfect temperature year-round." He opened his briefcase, pulled out her contract and tossed it on the soft-backed sofa near the pools. "Read through this while I get us a drink."

She gave the contract a rueful look. "You were that sure of me?"

"A dream is a powerful thing," he said simply. "So is desperation."

She opened her mouth as if to say something, then shut it after a long moment. *Bene.* She was learning.

"What can I get you to drink?"

"A glass of wine, thank you."

He pulled a bottle of rosé out of the wine fridge and tore off the foil.

"A toxicology screen?"

He had listed it as one of the up-front conditions. "Fairly standard, isn't it?"

"For a model with a history of *substance abuse*."

He worked the corkscrew into the bottle. "This is a five-million-dollar deal we're negotiating, Olivia. When a formerly trustworthy top model starts showing up late for her shoots…reneges on obligations…blows off a three-million-dollar contract, there has to be a reason. I'm covering my investment."

Her chin lifted at a defiant angle. "There was no substance abuse problem. Unless you call one dirty martini too many on the odd night out an issue."

"Alcohol is a drug. If it interfered with your work, it was an issue."

"It did *not* interfere with my work."

"Then what did?" He poured two glasses of the rosé, put the bottle back in the fridge and carried the glasses over to her. "For all intents and purposes, you were a client's dream until that last year. You did your work, you did it exceptionally well and you were conscientious. What happened to change all that? Why the out-of-control partying near the end?"

A stubborn look crossed her face. "Maybe I was getting my bad-girl genes out of my system. I am my mother's daughter after all."

"You were for the first part of your career, as well." He handed her a glass and sat down beside her.

She lifted a shoulder. "Maybe the glow faded. Maybe it wasn't enough to hold my attention anymore."

And maybe she was lying through her teeth. A model didn't just walk away from a three-million-dollar contract because she was bored. She fulfilled her obligations, left on good terms and used the contacts she had made to build her reputation as a designer.

It made no sense. It was a mystery he intended to unravel.

He pointed his glass at her. "Did you leave New York to get away from a man? Were there issues with a relationship?"

She gave him an even look. "There was only one relationship—a long-term one I had that ended on good terms before I left."

"With Guillermo Villanueva…"

"Yes."

One of the world's most sought-after photographers, Venezuelan-born Guillermo Villanueva was known for his ability to put a twist, a different angle, on a face or a landscape that had been shot a thousand times. He was equally known for his swarthy good looks, which had models flocking eagerly to his shoots, putting their best foot forward as he reduced them to fluttery, feminine creatures that bent to his will.

Had Olivia been like that with him, too?

"How long was the relationship?" he asked to distract himself from a question that didn't matter.

She gave him a pointed look. "Does this really have relevance here?"

"*Sì*, Olivia, it does. We're about to be in the spotlight as a newly engaged couple. I need to know your personal history."

She sighed. "Three years. We were together three years."

He blinked. An eternity as far as he was concerned… For him, a two-month stint with a woman was an accomplishment. He wondered if Villanueva had been unfaithful to her. It wouldn't be surprising given the opportunities the photographer would have had working with beautiful women day in, day out.

"Was Villanueva the reason for the partying?" he asked.

A glimmer of emotion flashed in her brilliant blue eyes. "Guillermo was the most steadying influence I had in my life."

"Then why leave him?"

She was silent for a long moment, her gaze resting on the cascading pools of water. "I fell out of love with him," she said finally. "I wasn't with him for the right reasons."

Her quiet, level voice held a poignancy that made him look at her hard. It was a pattern, it seemed, that she was with men for the wrong reasons. With Giovanni, it had been money, a mentor. With Villanueva? Maybe a mentor, also. A stepping-stone to bigger and better jobs?

His rancor stirred anew. He was suddenly very sorry for Guillermo Villanueva. He had likely never seen it coming, so blinded with the radiance that was Olivia. She, on the other hand, had been done with him, ready to take those last steps to stardom. And Villanueva had been left in the dust.

Rocco had seen it happen to his brilliant Sicilian friend Stefan with a woman he'd sacrificed everything for, only to find out she'd been more interested in his bank account than him. A more trusting man than the rest of the Columbia Four initially, Stefan had subsequently become ten times harder than all of them.

He grimaced, taking a healthy swallow of his wine. Love was like that. It was never equally distributed between two people. And the poor fool who didn't recognize that got his heart torn out eventually.

"Finish reading the contract," he instructed. "We have much to discuss."

She picked it up and scanned it. He wasn't expecting her to have issues with it. It was a straightforward, clean contract. Olivia's face and body would be exclusive to the House of Mondelli for the next twelve months in a five-million-dollar endorsement deal, after which the second part of the contract, a design partnership agreement, would kick in.

After a few moments, she tossed the contract on the coffee table. "It's fine. Minus the tox screen."

"Olivia…"

"No." Her voice was harsh. "You need to trust me. This is a two-way street."

He trusted her as much as his rogue stallion on his best-behaved day. About a centimeter leeway on the reins… But he needed to get this deal done.

"Bene." He inclined his head. "But one sign that I need to and I will do it, regardless of your objections." He flicked a hand at the contract. "Can your lawyer look at it tomorrow?"

"Yes. That shouldn't be a problem."

"I've also had the paperwork drawn up to release you from your Le Ciel contract. You can show him that, too. It will clear you of any remaining obligations."

She drew her bottom lip between her teeth. "Thank you. That's a big weight off my shoulders."

The vulnerability glittering in her eyes caught him off guard. It was there when you peeled back the layers. When she forgot to hide it. He studied her for a long moment, then told himself he'd be a fool to overanalyze it. To buy in to it.

"See that you don't let me down," he advised tersely. "The eyes of the world are going to be on us. Millions of dollars are at stake. Screw up *once*, miss one shoot by ten minutes, blow off an appearance, however insignificant, fail to show up to any job with less than one-hundred-percent enthusiasm and I will make you rue the day you put pen to paper."

An emotion he couldn't read flashed in her eyes. Intimidation? Fear? Antagonism?

Her gaze tangled with his. "I will execute this contract to the best of my ability. You have my word on it. See that you keep yours."

"I intend to do so." He rose to his feet, walked over to the bar, procured the wine bottle and refilled their glasses. "How does working alongside Mario Masini sound?"

Her eyes widened. "You're serious?"

He sat down and stretched his long legs out in front of him. "I never say anything I don't mean."

"Wow." She looked dumbstruck. And rightly so. Mondelli's head designer was a legend in the fashion industry. He had joined the company to partner with Giovanni when the two men were in their early twenties. His classic yet inspired designs were the mainstay of high-profile personalities worldwide who wanted a streamlined vision that took its cues from beautiful materials and perfect cuts.

He allowed an inner smile as his plan came to brilliant, vivid life. "So now we talk details. We have one year. I want to move fast on this."

She nodded, looking a little overwhelmed.

"There is a design conference in New York next week the House of Mondelli is represented at. You will come with me and we will announce you as the new face of Mondelli at the press conference on the opening day."

Her face went gray. "That's very fast."

"It's the perfect opportunity. The eyes of the design world will be there."

She pushed her hair out of her face in what he was coming to recognize as a nervous tick. "And the engagement? When do we announce that?"

"My plan is to let the gossip hounds do it. We go ring shopping tomorrow, we show up in New York together with a massive rock on your hand and let the buzz take care of the rest."

The gray cast to her skin deepened. "And your family? When will we tell them?"

"We'll have dinner with Alessandra tomorrow night and tell her. You have met her, *si*?"

She nodded. "We worked together on a shoot a few years ago."

"*Bene.* I am not intending on telling her the truth about us. She is too chatty, too apt to say the wrong thing to the wrong person. It's better she takes it for what it is."

She frowned. "Is our engagement really worth all this subterfuge? Wouldn't it be easier to simply announce me as the new face of Mondelli? It will generate a huge amount of buzz in its own right."

His gaze speared hers. "This is more than a publicity stunt, Olivia. This is the joining of two of the world's great brands. The creation of a dynasty, so to say. It will be a far more powerful story than you simply becoming the face of Mondelli."

"And when we *end* our engagement?"

"That will only increase the buzz. Everyone loves a heartsick, broken couple. It's great photography."

She looked at him as if he had an answer for everything. He did, in fact.

"I will have your belongings transferred to Villa Mondelli this week. I spend most of my time there commuting back and forth so it makes sense you are there with me. But we'll delay your actual move date until after we get back from New York. I have meetings in London later this week, and you likely won't want to spend your first days in the villa alone."

Her face lost the remainder of its color. "We're to live together?"

His mouth curved. "We're madly in love, Olivia. Of course we're living together."

"Yes, but—" she waved a hand at him "—we could position it as we're both so busy, I'm going to be traveling a ton, it just makes sense to keep it separate until we marry. I mean, living apart doesn't preclude..."

"A wild night in bed?" He shook his head. "Sorry to disappoint you, *bella*, but I'm not sleeping on your sofa to make this look real. You will move into Villa Mondelli when we get back."

She gave him an agitated look. "The apartment..."

He shrugged. "It's a good investment. If you can manage not to blow your money this time, maybe I'll allow you to buy it back."

Her mouth tightened. He plunged on relentlessly, "We have a lot of work to do before New York. Alessandra will be all about the big eyes for each other, but my Sicilian friend Stefan, who will undoubtedly want to toast us in New York, will be tougher. We'll need to know each other inside out."

She scrunched her face up. "What do you mean by tough?"

A wry smile twisted his mouth. "I went to Columbia with three other men I became very close with. We are all confirmed bachelors. For me to announce my engagement, to make such a quick, one-hundred-and-eighty-degree turn, we're going to have to make our feelings for each other convincing."

She slid a perfectly manicured nail in her mouth. "What will our story be, then?"

"I think we should say we met in a café and it was love at first sight."

She arched a brow at him, the humor of it all lost on her apparently. "And this was when?"

"A month ago. We've been staying out of the limelight, but now with your return to the modeling world, we're making our engagement public."

She chewed on the fingernail. *That* would have to stop, but he wasn't about to antagonize her further tonight. "Is there anyone you need to tell about the engagement?"

"My parents, eventually. I can do that in New York."

"You don't want to give them a heads-up?"

"We're not close," she said flatly. "It can wait."

"Siblings? Close friends? Anyone we should invite out the night we see Stefan?"

A shadow made its way across her face, intensifying the dark bags under her eyes. "No siblings," she said quietly. "And there are just the friends I've made here in Milan."

He nodded. "Any other details I should know?"

"No." She took a sip of her wine and lifted her gaze to his. "What else should I know about my fiancé other than the fact he is cynical and arrogant?"

"I work. A lot. Christian Markos and Zayed Al Afzal are my other two close friends I went to Columbia with. Christian is a financial genius based in Athens. Zayed has recently gone home to take the throne in his home country of Gazbiyaa."

"He's a *king*?"

"A sheikh. Gazbiyaa is in the heart of the Arabian desert."

"Okaaay." She rubbed a palm against her temple. "And Stefan? What does he do?"

"He's in high-end real estate. As in the deals that make

the *Wall Street Journal*... He doesn't touch anything under ten million."

She shook her head. "Quite the group of underachievers."

He lifted a shoulder. "We are all driven. But very different. More like brothers than friends. We even argue that way."

She smiled, and, *Dio*, when she did, it made the night sky light up. He'd have to make sure she didn't do that often. "You should know we run a charity together. It's a big thing for us. The Knights of Columbia was created to help disadvantaged youth overcome their backgrounds and succeed in business. It's based in New York, but we all do work in our home countries and funnel the kids through to various business programs in Manhattan." He took a sip of his wine. "We also personally mentor some of the kids."

Her eyes brightened. "It sounds amazing. Whose idea was it?"

"It arose out of work Christian was doing. He grew up on the streets of Athens, the child of a single mother. He never knew his father, had to fight his way out of poverty to take care of himself and his mother. It has defined him as a man, and he wanted to give back. We all loved what he was doing and wanted to be a part of it. Thus, the Knights of Columbia was born."

"I did charity work when I worked for Le Ciel," she murmured. "I miss it."

"We have a charity for young female designers who have suffered at the hands of men and have been forced to resort to shelters. It would be a great thing for you to get involved with if you have time."

"I would love to." She pressed her fingers against her mouth, her gaze uncertain. "You are so close to these men. How ever are we going to convince them this is real?"

An image of her plastered against the door of her apartment begging for more of him flashed through his head. His lip curled. "Act like you did that night in Navigli—act as if you want to devour me, as if you can't wait to get your hands on me. It doesn't get any more convincing than that."

A flush filled her cheeks. "That might be difficult," she drawled in response, "now that I know what kind of a man you are."

The insult bounced off him like the most ineffective of feints. "Fortunately, *cara*, pheromones aren't ruled by the brain. I'm sure you'll do just fine."

Her fingers tightened around the glass. He could tell she wanted to slap them across his face and tell him what to do with his deal. But she restrained herself because they both knew how important this was. For him, it was his chance to solidify control of House of Mondelli. For Olivia, her chance to take hold of her dream.

He only hoped he hadn't taken too big a risk on an asset that was a complete unknown. Because Olivia Fitzgerald was undoubtedly a wild card. She would either be the most brilliant play he'd ever orchestrated, or the one that would bring him down.

CHAPTER FIVE

OLIVIA TRIED TO maintain an air of enforced Zen as she and Rocco winged their way toward Manhattan in the Mondelli jet the following Sunday night, but with each mile the speedy little plane ate up toward the past she'd vowed to leave behind, her self-imposed calm faded further.

Her huge, square-cut, white-diamond engagement ring sat on her finger with an almost oppressive weight. It had already been pictured in tabloids and newspapers around the globe after she and Rocco had been spotted leaving an exclusive Via della Spiga boutique earlier that week. The taste of the media circus their engagement was about to become had already gone a long way toward ridding her of the ten pounds she needed to shed.

Technically, she was ready to face it. Her new wardrobe, courtesy of Mario Masini, was expertly packed in her suitcase stowed at the back of the jet. Her hair had been trimmed of its split ends, a shine added, her thoughts equally whipped into line by the Mondelli PR people, who'd key messaged her to within an inch of her life.

Outwardly she was perfect. Internally she was a mess.

She glanced over at her complex, stunning fiancé for a smidge of reassurance, but he had his head down working. Had been since they'd taken off seven hours ago.

She took advantage of the moment to study him. He may not be attracted to her, but she was to him, and he knew it. The way his tall, lithe body was too big for the streamlined airplane seat, the hard olive-skinned muscle visible where his shirtsleeves were rolled up to his elbows, the serious, intensely male lines of his face that always seemed to be furrowed in concentration, made her feel distinctly weak at the knees.

Pathetic, really, when he hadn't exercised any of those attributes on her since that kiss against her door, except for a few possessive touches during the dinner with Alessandra. She'd been sadly responsive to him, while he'd remained unaffected.

He also hated her. Let's not forget that. Reason number one to ignore him. He was an arrogant son of a bitch who thought she was a sycophant who'd bedded his *seventy-year-old* grandfather. She needed to get over him. *Now.*

She sighed and tapped her fingers on the glossy pages of the magazine lying on her lap. At least the massive amount of media coverage had negated the need to inform her parents of her engagement. Her mother had called her within minutes of reading the first tabloid piece, salivating over Rocco's money. Olivia had wanted to tell her she'd never see a penny of it, but Rocco had forbade her from revealing the truth to anyone. Which left her with exactly no one to confide in.

And God forbid she confide her feelings to her fiancé. Alessandra Mondelli, who'd been clearly fascinated with her brother's sudden engagement, clearly shocked to find Olivia hiding out in Milan and clearly determined to know all the details, had given her the lowdown on the man who seemed about as open as an ice cream shop on a bitterly cold February day.

"He's a driven perfectionist who's been forced his whole life to take charge," Alessandra had told her when Rocco had left their table in the busy Milanese restaurant to chat with a business acquaintance. "Of us when our father left, and of the company when Giovanni went running wild with his creative pursuits and left the business side of things in disarray." Alessandra had shaken her head. "He's hurting badly about Giovanni, but in typical Rocco fashion, he's internalized it all."

Alessandra's comments should have made Rocco seem more human, more approachable, but had instead only increased her insecurities. Yes, she was a world-famous beauty, but she was not her fiancé's type. He'd told her so.

That was supposed to help her heading into tonight's dinner with the formidable Stefan Bianco, who apparently had had his heart broken by a woman after his money?

Amazing.

She squirmed in her seat. Rocco glanced over at her, a sigh escaping his lips. "Are you always this distracted? You're like a six-year-old in need of toys…"

She rolled her eyes at how badly he read her. How completely inaccurately he'd judged her. To Rocco she was Mata Hari reincarnate.

"The paparazzi are going to be out in force looking for us," she murmured. "I'm anxious."

"Aren't you used to it by now?"

"Doesn't mean I have to like it." She pushed her hair out of her face. "I would have preferred an evening to acclimatize before I have to face it. It's intimidating enough having to convince one of your best friends we're mad about each other. Having a camera shoved in my face, I could do without."

His smile flashed white in the muted confines of the jet. "Worried you won't be able to control yourself?"

"From clawing your eyes out?" she came back tartly. "Yes."

The grooves on either side of his mouth deepened. "You know, I actually think we might pull this off. We argue like an old married couple."

She made a face. "Luckily this madness will end before that happens."

A curious gleam entered his eyes. "Do you ever intend to marry?"

"It isn't high on my list. I think I'll rely on my career as a designer instead."

His brow arched. "You don't want a big poufy dress and a veil? A lifetime commitment?"

"I'm not sure I'm capable of that kind of love."

Wow. She hadn't even realized she'd thought that until she'd said it.

He reclined back in his chair and fixed her with a speculative look. "That's an honest statement. One I can identify with."

"You don't think you are, either?"

His lips curled. "I don't *think* I'm not, I know I'm not. It's what makes this engagement of convenience just so very easy for me."

She wondered what had brought him to that conclusion. What was behind the cynicism Giovanni had spoken of when it came to his grandson… Despite his transgressions, Giovanni and his son had been madly in love with their wives. The Mondelli men clearly fell hard. So what had happened to Rocco? Had a woman burned him badly?

Their conversation was cut off as they made their final descent into Manhattan. The elegant little jet set down on the runway, they disembarked into the chill of a winter Manhattan night and were quickly ushered into a car operated by Rocco's driver and spirited to the Mondelli apartment in the heart of the city.

The insistent, pulsing energy of New York wrapped itself around her like a particularly deadly python with the ability to steal her breath. Her nerves began to shred as they navigated its busy streets and honking horns.

She had once adored this city, thrived on it as if it were

her lifeblood. Later, she had grown to hate it for what it had done to her, to the people she loved. Now her dominant emotion was fear. Fear of a debilitating variety.

Her chest as she stepped out of the limo in front of the Mondellis' exclusive Central Park West apartment building was so tight she felt as though they were on a smog alert times a million. She pressed a hand to the cool metal exterior of the car to steady herself. Rocco was by her side in a nanosecond, cupping her elbow.

"Are you all right?"

No, she wasn't all right. She'd never be all right again in this city.

But now was the time to pull herself together if she were to survive. She sucked in a deep breath, forced herself to nod and step away from the car. If she didn't think about Petra, if she didn't think about that last show at the Lincoln Center and how she'd disintegrated in front of her peers, she might just pull this off.

Rocco kept his hand under her elbow as he guided her into the limestone-faced building, notorious for its wealthiest-of-the-wealthy residents and the deal makers who anchored it with their vast fortunes. The doorman let them out on the twentieth floor, referring to Rocco by name as he wished them a good evening.

The apartment was beautifully decorated in muted caramels and greens, complementing the exquisite, original finish work the renovators had restored to a gleaming mahogany. Olivia headed straight for the long, narrow terrace that overlooked the park, braced her hands on the iron railing and sucked in big breaths, the chill in the air filling her lungs.

Rocco joined her, his jacket discarded, tie loosened. "What is it?" he asked quietly, throwing her a sideways glance. "What is it that upsets you so much about this city you were so triumphant in?"

The genuine concern on his face, the unusual softness in his voice, almost made her believe he cared. But letting her guard down around the man who held all the cards in this deal of theirs would be stupidity.

"It has some bad memories for me. I'm not the naive young girl making tons of money who couldn't see beyond the bright lights and the rush anymore."

His gaze rested on her face with that unnerving intensity he brought to everything. "Everyone has bad memories, Olivia. You can't let them control you."

"I'm not," she said brightly. "We're having dinner at an outrageously good restaurant, I get to meet the illustrious Stefan Bianco and I'm about to become a household name again. Who could ask for more?"

She spun on her heel and strode inside. The first thing she noticed upon further investigation of the luxury apartment was that there was only one bedroom in the suite.

They were sharing a bed.

Oh, Lord. She glanced around desperately. Maybe there was a pullout sofa.

"Only one bed," Rocco qualified, coming to a halt behind her. "Sorry, *princessa*. This apartment wasn't meant for entertaining."

Compartmentalize, she told herself. She needed to compartmentalize this problem and focus on the big one at the moment: getting ready for this dinner she so heartily didn't want to attend. She glanced at the grandfather clock ticking loudly in the lounge, and her queasiness dissolved into panic. They had to leave in fifteen minutes.

She hightailed it into the bathroom. Luckily she was adept at putting on her face in just under seven minutes. Her hair, a bit wild from the travel, would have to be put up in a quick chignon. And her dress...

Which dress?

She kicked off her jeans and top and raced into the dressing room. The breath was knocked from her lungs when she ran headfirst into a brick wall, otherwise known as Rocco searching for a tie. His hands closed automatically around her waist to steady her. Winded, she put a palm to his chest and caught her breath. The feel of warm, muscled male beneath her fingertips upped her pulse a point or two. *Damn.*

She unpeeled herself from him and put some space between them. "So sorry," she murmured with a self-conscious smile. "I'm working on eight minutes."

He nodded and stood back to give her space. The heightened color in his high cheekbones was a rare enough sight that she stopped and stared for a moment. *What's wrong with him?*

She followed his gaze like a detective searching for clues. Down over her chest it went, past her hips, down her legs. And it struck her then. She was wearing lingerie. Skimpy lingerie. It was so second nature for her to run around half-naked given her former profession—*current profession*, she corrected—that she hadn't given it a second thought.

The color darkening his olive skin deepened. Her brain mind-numbingly processed the facts in front of her. That was lust on his face. Unmistakable. He had been lying to her.

Her mind reeled with the realization. He didn't want to admit he wanted her because he didn't want to want her. And wasn't she an idiot for ignoring her instincts? She had *known* that night in Navigli the heat hadn't been one-sided. And yet he'd cruelly let her think he found her lacking in the face of his Italian brunettes!

"You…" She bit her lip before she tore a strip off him, her rational brain kicking in. Having one up on the man who held all the cards could be a good thing.

"Could you help me with my dress?" she asked sweetly instead, turning her back to him as she rustled through her suitcase for one of Mario's dresses that eluded wrinkles. "That would speed things up."

Rocco stood utterly still as Olivia bent over in front of him and rustled through the case. The lingerie she had on were not the skimpiest he had ever seen, but on his blonde bombshell of a fiancée they looked indescribable. Her rounded, toned behind made his head feel as tight as his groin. Her legs went on forever, ending in slim perfect ankles he could so clearly imagine wrapped around himself he almost groaned.

She spun around, holding up a silver-blue dress victoriously. "Just need you to do the hook at the back."

Or he could hang himself right now. That was a definite option. Better than seeing her perfect nipples outlined against the fine lace of her bra. Better than wondering how soft the skin was between those delectable thighs, showcased perfectly by the revealing cut of her panties...

"Rocco?" She waggled a brow at him. "Are you okay?"

"Perfetto." He waved a hand at her. "Put the damn dress on so I can do it up. The driver's waiting outside."

Mercifully, she slipped the dress over her head. It didn't get any easier, though, as she backed up against him and held her hair out of the way for him to do up the clasp. "That top tiny one please."

He found the tiny hook, his big hands fumbling over the minute closure. She squeezed closer to him, the silk of her dress swishing against his thighs, sending his blood pressure into dangerous territory.

"You smell good." She sighed. "What are you wearing?"

With her bottom perilously close to his raging erection, her lush body lining the length of his, there was only one thought in his head and it wasn't the name of the cologne he was wearing.

The hook slid into the clasp. He uttered a silent prayer of thanks. *"Finito."*

She turned around, a tiny smile playing about her lips. *"Grazie.* I may need help taking it off again later, though."

He would be conveniently getting ice for a nightcap at that moment. He grabbed the tie he wanted to wear, did it up with swift precision while Olivia did her hair, then ushered her out into the warm night air and to the car.

Stefan Bianco met them at the back entrance of the fusion restaurant he was part owner of in Chelsea. His friend's mouth curved into one of his signature lazy smiles when he saw them, the one that camouflaged one of the most ruthless, hard-edged businessmen Rocco had ever met.

He and Rocco embraced.

"Welcome to Tempesta Di Fuoco."

"Impressive, my friend." Rocco stood back and drew Olivia forward. "Olivia, meet Stefan. Not nearly as intimidating as he's made out to be."

Stefan carried the hand Olivia offered to his lips. "You are even more beautiful in person. I can see why Rocco lost his head."

A hint of color washed his fiancée's cheeks. "And you are even more…charismatic…than Rocco painted you."

Amusement gleamed in Stefan's eyes. "You will have to enlighten me on his description. I'm sure it would be entertaining."

Rocco curved an arm around Olivia's waist and pulled her into his side. "Nothing you haven't heard before, *fratello.*"

They were seated at a quiet table in one of the alcoves of the exceedingly modern restaurant, done in chrome and steel and muted colors. Rocco and Olivia sat on one side of the table for four, while Stefan sat on the other, his hand lifting to summon the sommelier to bring them a very old, very fine bottle of cabernet.

"I trust that's fine?" he asked Olivia. "I can't tolerate champagne. Such a woman's drink. And French," he added caustically.

"I'm not a fan of champagne myself," Olivia observed, bestowing that high-wattage smile of hers on his friend. "And I do love a good Cab, thank you."

Stefan did a double take. There wasn't a man on this earth who would be immune to Olivia Fitzgerald when she used that smile on him, and Rocco would bet his stock portfolio by the end of this meal she would have his incorrigible friend eating out of her hand.

Stefan sat back and crossed his arms over his chest. "So how did you manage to work your way past my friend's considerable defenses? He has enough to man an army."

A smile curved Olivia's lips. "He picked me up in a café after scaring my girlfriends away... It was more... lust than love at first sight."

Humor darkened his friend's eyes. "That sounds more like him. What *isn't* like him is to fall flat on his face like this. He's usually much more careful. I always said *if* he'd ever marry, he would choose a blue-blooded Italian to carry on the Mondelli line and live a very premeditated life."

Olivia blinked at the backhanded compliment. Rocco put up his hand. "I'm still here, *fratello*, in case you'd forgotten."

His friend shrugged. "You have to admit, this is knee-jerk behavior for you. If we were in my wine cellar, you'd spend half an hour choosing the vintage, then decide perhaps it needed more thinking on."

Olivia put her water down with a deliberate movement, those amazing blue eyes of hers glittering as she recovered. Rocco almost jumped out of his seat when she curved her palm around his thigh underneath the table and squeezed. "Apparently we are compatible on other levels. Although Rocco attempted to deny it at first."

A muscle jumped in his jaw at the twin sensations of

Olivia's hand burning into his thigh like a brand and the anger emanating from her like a physical, living entity despite the smile plastered across her face.

"There was a slight miscommunication between us at first," he managed. "We moved past it."

Olivia's fingers splayed wider on his thigh, caressing muscles far too alert from that close encounter in the dressing room.

Stefan's gaze sharpened on his fiancée. "That was you at Giovanni's funeral."

Olivia nodded. "Rocco and I had had a lover's quarrel. Not the most appropriate place, I admit, but he was green with jealousy over my former relationship with Guillermo Villanueva. I managed to convince him there's simply nothing left there."

"There's a first." Stefan's mouth quirked. "I'm not sure I've ever seen Rocco care enough about a female to go running after her."

Rocco gritted his teeth, unable to remove Olivia's disturbing hand because *his* right hand was covering hers on the table. He squeezed it hard. "I did not *run* after you."

"Of course you did, sweetheart." She gave him a saccharine-sweet smile and closed her fingers over his thigh in another firm squeeze. "You showed up on my doorstep with flowers and poetry." She angled a look at Stefan. "Can you imagine big bad Rocco writing poetry? It was outrageously cute. Anyway," she said, looking adoringly back at her fiancé, "he really had nothing to worry about. He knows I only have eyes for him."

A hot flush spread its way across his cheeks. His brain was catching up with his groin now, and it hit him what was happening. Olivia had read his attraction in that dressing room, had figured out he was lying. And this was payback.

He released her hand and captured the one on his thigh,

bringing it to his lips. "I do know that, *amore mio*. Now stop spilling our secrets. I'll never be able to live them down."

"On the contrary," Stefan demurred, "I am highly entertained."

Rocco kept a firm grip on his fiancée's hand. "Olivia is enough to inspire any man to poetry." He couldn't mask the sarcasm in his voice. "I'm sure you can see how that is."

Stefan's green eyes danced. "I certainly can. Maybe you should read the poem at the wedding. I'm sure we'll all be wiping the tears away."

Rocco gave his friend a dangerous look. He was saved by the arrival of the sommelier, who presented the wine to Stefan. The Sicilian glanced at the label, nodded and indicated for it to be served.

"So when and where is this star-studded marriage expected to happen?" he asked. "Are you giving yourselves some time to enjoy your newfound *compatibility*, or should we expect an invitation?"

Olivia tucked in closer to Rocco's side and returned her hand to his thigh. "We haven't set a date. It's going to be an extremely busy year for both of us. Maybe the summer of next year."

Stefan nodded. "Nothing wrong with restraint. *Bambini* can come later."

Rocco almost choked on his mouthful of water. "I haven't totally gone off the deep end, Bianco. There's been no talk of *bambini* yet."

Olivia's fingers settled in a red-light zone between his thighs. His erection throbbed in his pants, begging for more. "Oh, but we don't plan to wait too long, do we, *cara*? I *am* twenty-six. These eggs of mine aren't getting any younger."

Rocco gave her a meaningful smile laced with warning. "They've plenty of life left in them, *bella*. You *are* only twenty-six. And believe me, I do want you to myself for a while."

Tonight. To strangle her. To find out what had happened to the nerve-racked woman he'd arrived in New York with.

Olivia stared innocently back at him, using her big doe eyes to full effect. "Oh, I want that, too. I know what we've agreed upon, sweetheart… It's just that when I think of little Roccos with dark curly hair and big brown eyes, I find it hard to resist."

"Who could?" Stefan drawled facetiously. "If we populated the world with millions of little Roccos, it would be a better place."

"And the hands…" Olivia picked one of his up and showed it off. "Rocco has great hands, but they'll be chubby little amazing ones to begin with."

Stefan nodded. "No doubt about it. Mondelli has great hands. Many a woman would attest to that, but now that he's taken, too bad for them, hmm?"

Rocco bit down on the inside of his mouth. Counted to three. "I am famished," he asserted in a blatant change of subject. "Should we look at the menu?"

"The chef has prepared a special celebratory meal." Stefan eliminated that distraction with a wave of his hand and a glimmer of laughter in his dark eyes. "Sit back and enjoy."

Rocco attempted to. The vibe in Stefan's new restaurant was high energy, the food as they tasted their appetizers superb, the easy familiarity of the conversation with his longtime friend enjoyable. It was Olivia who was the problem. If she'd been sitting any closer to him she'd be in his lap. Her spicy perfume, which he found he enjoyed a bit too much, kept invading his thinking processes. And her hands were *everywhere*… Caressing his fingers on the table, massaging his thigh. And now she'd slipped her shoe off and was—what did the Americans call it? *Playing footsie* with him!

Santo Cielo.

He frowned and focused intently on the idea Stefan was proposing for a Knights of Columbia charity basketball game fund-raiser. "I think it fits perfectly with our mission statement," he agreed. "And if you can get the players, we're golden. When were you thinking?"

Stefan lifted a brow. "I just told you—late September so we can play outside."

He closed his eyes briefly as Olivia's inquisitive fingers investigated the contents of his pocket, then slid back out again. "Right. Sorry."

"Can I help?" Olivia leaned forward, all halo-endowed innocence. "I'm in my element at a fund-raiser. I can cheer you on."

Rocco watched his friend keep his eyes above her plunging neckline. *Just.* "By all means," Stefan said wryly. "Half the men in New York would show up to see you." He passed his palm over the heavy stubble on his chin. "Would you consider doing a promotional poster for us?"

"No, she wouldn't," Rocco inserted. "My fiancée is not a pinup model."

"She was."

"It's true," Olivia offered. "I don't mind. Those were fun shoots."

"No." The word exploded out of his mouth as Olivia slid her finger up the zipper of his pants and traced the rigid length of him. He was on fire. Literally on fire. He reached down, picked up her hand and slapped it down on her thigh, then rose from the table.

"I need to make a call." He directed the words at Stefan. "Entertain my fiancée, would you?"

"That won't be difficult." Stefan's amused comment sidled through the air to him as he walked away.

He exited the front door of the restaurant and stood leaning against the facade of the building while he made his call, his only company on the street another diner in a designer suit smoking a cigarette. When he finished, he stayed there for a moment, breathing in the fresh air. Attempting to regain control over his tense, aroused body.

Stefan strolled out the front door and over to where he stood. "Cooling off? Where was her hand, by the way?"

Rocco gave him a dark look. "Where is she?"

"In the ladies'." Stefan moved his gaze over him and shook his head. "She has your number, my friend. You have it bad. I feel as if I'm watching Rocco unplugged."

He wanted badly to tell his friend it was a facade. That *she*, Olivia, was playing a necessary role. Trying to drive him mad while she was at it… But he couldn't risk everything he'd put into this investment by being anything less than fully committed. Blood brothers or otherwise.

He pulled on the cloak of aloofness he did every bit as well as Stefan. "She is a handful. But honestly," he challenged, quirking a brow at his friend, "would you want anything else?"

Stefan eyed him. "Perhaps not. I guess I'm wondering if the board's POV on you has anything to do with this sudden engagement."

His insides tensed. "You think I care what they think?"

Stefan leaned back against the wall beside him. "I'm just saying marriage is a big step. This is all very sudden." He waved a hand at him. "So she's beautiful. So she's good in bed. Those are a dime a dozen for you, *fratello*. Enjoy her, but think hard about what you're doing."

Rocco turned to face him. Wondered why he felt the unusual urge to put his fist through his friend's face. "She's a good choice for me and for the brand."

"Maybe. But you're grieving over your grandfather. Give yourself some time before you do something stupid."

"That's why we're planning a long engagement." Rocco

gave the Sicilian an assessing look. "When are *you* going to get over Serena? No one wants to say it, but it's time."

The guarded, impenetrable expression that seemed to be his friend's de facto look of late descended over his square-jawed face. "I've been over Serena for a long time."

"You think so?"

Stefan stared him down. "You think *you're* in control of your little situation in there?"

No. He decidedly was not. But he was about to fix that.

The deliberate twist of the key in the lock of the apartment door echoed excessively loudly in Olivia's ears after the loaded silence in the car coming home. The explosive look on Rocco's face as they'd driven through the relatively quiet streets of Manhattan made her wonder if she'd taken her exercise in distraction a bit too far.

He stood back for her to enter, his long, lean body taut, his face so blank that adrenaline pounded through her in a disconcerting rush. Hadn't she done her job? She'd really gotten into her role as fiancée. Even Stefan had seemed to enjoy himself… And she hadn't thought about tomorrow's press conference even once, which was an added bonus.

The door slammed shut. She winced and turned to face him.

"What the *hell* was that?" he growled, his stance open-legged and aggressive.

She touched her fingers to her throat. "I was having some fun. This really is a ridiculous situation, Rocco. Stefan wasn't going to believe it was love at first sight for one second. I was trying to make it believable."

His long strides carried him to her so quickly the room seemed to sway around her. He stopped mere inches from her, the heat pulsing from him so intensely she felt it singe her skin. "You weren't trying to make it *believable*. You were trying to drive me nuts. Stefan thinks I've lost it."

She bit her lip, her gaze skipping away from his. "I'm sorry. I might have taken it a bit too far."

"A bit too far?" Incredulity dug a furrow across his brow. "You had your hand on my crotch."

Heat rushed to her cheeks. "I said I went too far. I've apologized."

His gaze bored into hers. "Sorry isn't an effective response for what I'm feeling right now, *tesoro*. I am *way* past the line."

Of what? Her throat went dry, her stomach clenching in a knot. "You lied to me. You told me you weren't attracted to me that night in Navigli when you clearly were."

"For a *reason*."

Her hands clenched by her sides. "Because you think I was with Giovanni."

"Because you *were* with Giovanni."

She made a sound in the back of her throat. "Do you really know your grandfather *so little* you think he would have been having an affair with a woman young enough to be his granddaughter?"

"He was not in his right mind." A muscle ticked in his jaw, a flare of fury firing in his eyes. "He was off in some…fairy-tale land of late. Doubtless you perpetuated that."

Her head pounded with fury. "You are so wrong, you know that? So laughably wrong. And you know what else? You deserved that tonight, Rocco. And more, if I were to be honest. You can't even admit the truth to yourself about how you feel."

He stared at her, long and hard, his face contorting into an expression that made her want to head for the door and run. "Here I am, then, Olivia," he rasped, his gaze impaling hers. "About ten showers away from finding your payback amusing. And that *is* the truth." A muscle in his jaw ticked wildly. "You want to finish what you started? Put your hand back where it was, *cara.* In fact, put more than your hand there." His voice softened to a low purr. *"I dare you."*

The heat, the potent attraction that had been smoldering, building, between them all night wrapped itself around her like a shroud, seizing her lungs. Despite what he thought of her, despite what he'd done to her that night in Navigli, her body wanted him to finish what he'd started. Badly.

She raised her gaze to his. Dark color stained his high cheekbones, everything about him hard, masculine challenge. He would be spectacular in bed. All that intensity caged in an outrageously good body. She could almost taste how good he would be.

She nearly did it, too. Because numbing her brain as to what lay ahead just a little bit longer was high on her agenda. Then her rational brain kicked in. Short-term avoidance wasn't going to help her in reality. She stepped back, removed herself from all that heat and called it a brush with insanity.

"No, thank you, Rocco. I'm finally starting to learn the rules of your game, and I decline. This year is going to be hard enough without introducing sex into the mix."

She watched him process her response. The emotion that flickered through his volatile gaze. Watched him firmly slam a lid on it. "I tend to wholeheartedly agree. But push me again like that, Olivia, and I won't be responsible for my actions, deal or not. Count on that."

A shiver rocked through her. She turned and walked into the bedroom before the madness escalated. She should be focusing on the day ahead, figuring out how she was going to get through it rather than allowing herself to become hopelessly distracted with Rocco.

Not that anything could prepare her for returning to the life she'd left behind. Nothing ever could.

CHAPTER SIX

IT WAS A New York press frenzy at its finest, camera people crawling over one another to get a better position, journalists jockeying their way to the front of the room, extralarge coffee cups clutched in their hands. The buzz of a big story was in the air.

"No doubt way over the fire code," Savanna Piers, Mondelli's chic head of public relations, commented wryly, "but no one's going anywhere."

Olivia stood alongside Savanna and Rocco in the atrium of the hotel where the annual meeting of fashion designers was being held, the opening press conference about to begin. Standing beside them were spokespeople from the other represented manufacturers, but it was clear from the tone of the overheard conversations nobody wanted to talk to them. They all wanted to talk to *her*: Olivia Fitzgerald, the supermodel who had abandoned her career at its peak, defected on a three-million-dollar contract with a major French cosmetics company and disappeared from the face of the earth.

A sheen of perspiration blanketed her body. She felt a pool of it trickle down her back. Felt her breathing quicken as the oxygen in the room seemed to drain with every second...

The colors and movement around her faded into a detailless swirling gray. It reached out for her then, the panic, beckoning her, dark and familiar. She pulled in a desperate breath and fought it. Tried to hold it at bay, but the room grew darker around her.

"I need some air." She backed away and headed toward the hallway. Standing with her back against the wall in the corridor as catering staff bustled by her, she closed her eyes and made herself breathe in and out, deep long breaths like her therapist had taught her.

Eleven years she'd been having these panic attacks. Since she was fifteen. And they never got less terrifying. On the road in foreign countries with no support system in her emotionally unavailable parents and the stress of having to be the best every time she stepped onto a set, they'd started one night in Berlin. Debilitating, overwhelming, she'd been terrified of them. It had felt as though she was losing her mind.

Petra had finally made her see a doctor. Her therapist had helped her get the attacks somewhat under control, but when the pressure was high she couldn't fight them. Like that night at the Lincoln Center. It had ended her career.

"Olivia."

Rocco had joined her in the hallway. She opened her eyes to look at him, but the world kept swaying around her and she closed them again.

"There was no air in there."

He took her hands in his and pulled her down into a squatting position. "Head between your knees."

She pushed her head down and breathed. But it didn't seem as if she could get enough air into her lungs... The blackness was calling to her. Comforting. Easier than being here.

Rocco's hands tightened around hers. "No. Don't do that. Breathe, Olivia. Deep breaths, in and out."

His hands were tight around her ice cold ones. *Insistent.* She kept breathing, in and out. Deep, steadying pulls of air into her lungs. And slowly the blackness receded.

She brought herself upright. Rocco's gaze was pinned on her, dark and concerned. "Better?"

"Yes."

He glanced at his watch. "We're starting in five minutes. Are you okay to go back in?"

She nodded.

He brought her to her feet with a hand around her waist and kept a firm palm to her back as they walked back inside. Savanna led them to the side of the podium, her eagle-eyed gaze resting on Olivia's face. "Focus on the feel-good story of you and Rocco and your partnership. No one's going to choose mean over a picture-perfect story if they have any sense. You're America's sweetheart. Go with it."

Was. She had been America's sweetheart... Now she was afraid *sensational* was going to rule the day.

She straightened the hem of her dress as the president of this year's conference took the stage and made his opening remarks. By the time Mondelli was summoned forward, Olivia's knees were knocking against one another. Rocco captured her hand in his and started up the steps to the podium. The room blurred into a sea of faces and electronics as she climbed the steps, her clammy fingers clutching tighter to Rocco's as they ascended.

"Relax," he murmured out of the side of his mouth, giving her hand a squeeze. "I'm right here with you."

Despite her ever-present antagonism toward him, she *did* feel better with him by her side. Rocco was like that tree in a storm you knew would never come down. Its roots were too secure, its foundation too solid, to ever be unearthed by a mere media scrum.

Reporters began yelling questions even before they reached the microphone. Rocco held up a hand to silence them. "If you'll let me make my announcement, there will be plenty of time for questions."

When the din finally cleared, Rocco tugged on her hand

and drew her to the microphone. "I know you have all missed her, which is why I am thrilled to welcome Olivia Fitzgerald back to the modeling world as the new face of the House of Mondelli."

The room broke out in a fevered pitch. Rocco held up a hand and silenced them. "Combining the talents of one of the world's most famous faces with one of the globe's most venerable fashion houses is an undeniably exciting occasion to mark. But," he added, slipping an arm around Olivia's waist and tucking her into his side, "as many of you have speculated, there is another union we are even more happy to announce, and that is the forthcoming marriage of Olivia and I."

The noise in the room grew deafening. Savanna stepped forward and took control of the Q and A. "Francesca," she called out, pointing to an older blond-haired fashion reporter from one of the networks.

"First of all," Francesca began, "congratulations on your engagement and partnership." Her gaze shifted to Olivia. "The mystery we're all trying to unravel, Olivia, is why you disappeared at the peak of your career. Would you care to set the record straight?"

Olivia swallowed hard. *Why couldn't they just let the past lie?*

"It's very simple." She forced the words through excessively dry lips. "I just needed some time away. I was working on a project I'm going to be very excited to tell you about shortly."

The veteran reporter lifted a brow. "You reneged on a three-million-dollar contract with Le Ciel to *take some personal time*?"

Her heart dropped. *Here we go.*

"That contract has now been settled," she said huskily. "For legal reasons, I have to leave it at that."

"Word is," Francesca continued, undaunted, "Le Ciel is

furious. Do you think this will impact your career going forward?"

Olivia felt some of her old press savvy kick back in. "I was just named the face of Mondelli. Does it look like it?"

The veteran reporter inclined her head with a wry smile.

"Where were you hiding out?" The question came from the center of the room.

"I was in Milan." She threw a smile at her fiancé. "Where I met Rocco."

Savanna pointed to another veteran fashion reporter. "Dan."

"When will we first see Olivia in your campaigns?"

"In the spring," Rocco answered. "You'll see her back in New York for Fashion Week next month."

Savanna nodded at a redhead Olivia didn't recognize, wearing very fashionable purple glasses. "Tara?"

"How is the House of Mondelli going to move forward without Giovanni's genius at the helm? Some say Mario won't be enough to keep things afloat."

"We have half a dozen spectacular young designers Giovanni trained working with Mario," Rocco said smoothly. "No company can be content to rest on its laurels. We had always intended these designers to carry the torch forward. Giovanni was seventy after all."

"Olivia." A notoriously bigmouthed gossip reporter waved from the front. "How does it feel to land one of the world's most sought-after bachelors?"

Olivia relaxed back into Rocco's arm and turned to smile up at him. "Very lucky."

Eyes glittering with humor, Rocco lifted a hand to cup her jaw. "I am the lucky one to *land*, as you put it, Olivia."

"Since you've managed to elude us for the past week," the gossip reporter continued, "how about a kiss?"

Her fiancé let loose a good-natured smile. "I suppose that's only fair."

Her heartbeat picked up in a steady thrum as Rocco splayed his fingers wider around her jaw, leaned down and covered her lips with his own. Her lashes fluttered closed as he took her mouth in a thorough kiss that had the camera flashes going off madly like fireworks.

She was just off balance enough when he set her away from him to much applause from the scrum that the next question hit her from left field.

"Olivia. Can you tell us what happened that night at the Lincoln Center? What caused your meltdown?"

She froze, her face suspended midsmile. Frederic, the producer of the show that night at the Lincoln Center, an old personal friend of hers, had swiftly replaced her when she'd faltered and hadn't been able to take the stage. He'd forbidden any talk of what had happened afterward on pain of his influential wrath. But apparently someone had talked.

How much did they know?

The room started to sway dangerously around her, perspiration sliding down her back in rivulets now. Air got harder to pull in, but she sucked it in desperately, the question echoing over and over in her head. Scenes from that night flashed through her brain—ugly, paralyzing, stomach churning...

"Olivia?" Rocco set a supporting palm to the small of her back. The touch sent words tumbling out of her mouth.

"It was very hot backstage that evening," she rasped. "I was not feeling well."

Rocco started proactively detailing some of the key campaign elements they would see from Mondelli in the spring/summer. She managed to plaster a smile on her face as their time ran out and Rocco thanked the media. But it wasn't over. It was never going to be over.

Three hours and an excruciatingly boring reception later, Rocco shoved a glass of brandy into the hand of a still blank-faced Olivia in the quiet stillness of their apartment salon, and tried to contain his growing frustration. Neither he nor Savanna had been able to get his fiancée to talk after the press conference, despite their repeated attempts to discover what she was hiding. No one thought it was going to end there, and preempting whatever was to come was the best strategy. Unfortunately, his fiancée wasn't talking.

Can you tell us what happened that night at the Lincoln Center, Olivia? What made you have a meltdown?

The reporter's question rang in his head. No doubt Olivia hadn't been the most reliable model in the final couple of years she'd worked, but she'd never been billed a prima donna. So what had the reporter meant? What had happened that night?

He had a feeling it was the key to everything, the key to Olivia, yet no one was talking, not even Frederic Beaumont, the man who had produced the show that night, deflecting Rocco's inquiry at tonight's reception with a lifted brow. "As your fiancée said, it was extremely hot backstage. A lot of the models were struggling."

Closing ranks. He didn't believe him for one minute.

He glanced at his mute fiancée, grabbed his own tumbler and paced the room. "I can't help you if you won't talk to me."

Olivia pushed the brandy aside, her face white and pinched as she sat curled up in his favorite reading chair. "I don't want your help. It's ancient history."

"In case you hadn't noticed," he disputed heatedly, "it came back to life today. You are a very expensive asset of mine, Olivia. You think they're going to let whatever it is lie? Tell me what it is and we'll deal with it together."

She gave him another one of those blank looks. "You heard what I said. I wasn't feeling well. End of story."

He eyed her with growing ire. "The reporter referred to it as a meltdown."

"Reporters like to make things dramatic that aren't."

He muttered an oath beneath his breath. "And the reason you fell apart when the question was asked?"

She pressed her lips together. "I am frustrated. I just wish people would leave it alone and stop prying into my personal life when it's none of their business."

His free hand fisted at his side, his five-million-dollar investment pounding in his head. He counted to three, forced out a long breath and went to kneel by her chair. "I want to help you, Olivia. Give me *something*. It can't just have been the heat that night."

She pushed her spine back into the chair, recoiling away from him. "You want to protect an *asset*. Rest assured, Rocco, I will not renege on our deal, and I will perform the duties of my contract *to the letter*."

"This isn't just about you being an asset. You are struggling... I can help."

Her sapphire eyes heated to a dark blue flame. "Like you wanted to help me when you seduced me that night in Navigli to find out what kind of a woman I was? Like you wanted to help me when you coerced me into a return to modeling you knew I didn't want? Better we both do our jobs, Rocco, and refrain from pretending we care when we don't."

He almost would have bought her bravado had it not been for the wounded, vulnerable glint in her eyes. The pallor in her skin. The look she'd had all day that a slight breeze might knock her over. Her fiery gaze spoke of fear and pain and, most of all, a bone-deep sadness that got to him despite his efforts to remain detached.

He rose, sat on the edge of the chair and caught her chin in his fingers to turn her gaze to his. *"Tell me."*

He was surprised at the tenderness in his voice. At an empathy he hadn't known he possessed. She blinked and stared at him. *Dio*, this woman did something to him. It didn't matter she had been his grandfather's, that Giovanni's body wasn't even cold in his grave and still he wanted to comfort her. Touch her. He wanted to carry her to bed and make love to her and banish those demons from her eyes.

Madness. Pure madness.

The far too perceptive Stefan Bianco had had it right. Olivia did have his number. She had always had his number, right from that first night in Navigli.

Her gaze connected with his and read what lay there. Confusion darkened her vibrant blue orbs.

"Rocco…"

Her husky, hesitant tone prompted the return of his sanity. She had never been, nor would she ever be, his. *Impossible.*

He stood up with an abrupt movement. "Drink the brandy," he muttered roughly. "I will order us dinner."

When he'd finally sent an exhausted Olivia to bed and sat on the terrace with a final brandy in his hand, he was glad for the city that never slept. The honking horns and peeling ambulances kept him company, floodlit Central Park a feast for the senses as he tipped his head back and drank it in.

The silence, the solitude, grounded him as it always did. Made his present situation crystallize like the stars emerging from the silvery haze in the cloudy night sky above.

The more distance he kept from the woman inside who was driving him mad, the better. It had taken him hours last night to wrestle his body into an acceptable enough state to get into bed, after which the scent of her had driven him half-crazy. He'd been out of bed at 5:00 a.m. out of the pure need, *not* to look at his sultry fiancée splayed across his bed, glorious hair everywhere.

But it was more than that. This restlessness in him came from a place he was loath to face. He was bitterly afraid he had been wrong about Olivia. Very wrong.

She had clearly been lying just now, as she had during the press conference. The shut-down, blank look on her face had said it all. Which pointed out an uncomfortable fact. He'd never seen that look on her face before. Not when she'd denied Giovanni was her lover that night in Milan after he'd seduced her. Not through this past trying week when he'd plied her with a million questions to get their stories and backstory straight. She had always told him the truth, however painful, or she hadn't said anything at all.

Until tonight. Until today at the press conference. He could tell the difference. He could read her now.

Do you really know your grandfather so little you think he would have been having an affair with a woman young enough to be his granddaughter?

He ran his palm over the stubble on his jaw, a jolt of unease slicing through him. Giovanni not giving him sole control of Mondelli had shaken him, made him question how well he knew the man who had raised him, who had been his heart and soul. But Giovanni was also a complex man with many layers. Perhaps there were facets of him he hadn't known. Perhaps he *had* had an affair with Tatum Fitzgerald.

Tonight when he'd had that chat with Frederic Beaumont, the wily old Frenchman had congratulated him on capturing the "most enchanting creature he'd ever worked with" in Olivia, and made a veiled comment about Mondelli men having a thing for Fitzgerald women. When Rocco had lifted a brow at the comment, Frederic had only said sagely that Tatum Fitzgerald had been one of Giovanni's great muses, but his eyes had said much more.

He took a swig of the brandy, closing his eyes as its warmth heated his insides. If his grandfather had engaged in an out-of-character affair with Tatum Fitzgerald, that was one thing. But to have an affair with her daughter, as well? It didn't sit right in his chest. Maybe it never had.

He'd been so angry at his grandfather's death when he'd confronted Olivia, he'd wanted to lash out, and she had been the most convenient target. Brand her a gold digger and make himself feel better by solving the problem.

The uneasy feeling inside him intensified. Propelled him out of his chair and to the railing, Manhattan glistening below in all its finery. What if he'd been wrong? What if he'd branded the woman sleeping in his bed an opportunist when she had really been Giovanni's inspiration in the most innocent sense? When perhaps *she* had been the one to reinvigorate a creativity that had begun to fail the aging genius? He had seen it in those designs…

He took another sip of the brandy. The spirit blazed an undeniable path of self-awareness through him. Had he wanted to think the worst of Olivia because of just how very much she got to him? How she'd managed to penetrate the ironclad exterior he'd adopted the day he'd realized his father as he'd known him was never coming back? When he'd decided no one would ever get to him emotionally again?

Sandro had only been twenty-seven when his wife of the same age had died giving birth to Alessandra. Suffering from severe preeclampsia, Letizia had delivered him a healthy baby girl, but stolen his one true love in the process. His father had fallen apart, descended into a grief so raw it had scared his two children witless and left them with no one but each other.

At first, Giovanni had been patient with his son. Had turned a blind eye to Sandro's drinking, to his gambling, but after a time, when he'd decided enough was enough, that Sandro's children needed a father and he needed his son back at Mondelli, Sandro had said he'd needed more time. Then more. Until it became clear he couldn't mentally handle a return to the family business, until he'd gambled Rocco's family home away and it had become apparent he wasn't capable of taking care of his children, either. Of himself.

Rocco could remember the day vividly when Giovanni had arrived at their house, soon to be taken by creditors, and ordered him and Alessandra to gather their things. He'd only been seven and a half at the time, but he would never forget the anguish in his father's eyes as his grandfather had scooped them up and took them home to Villa Mondelli, his disappointment in his son palpable in the older man's demeanor.

Rocco had absorbed his father's anguish, the hint of madness that losing his mother had instilled in him, and although he had been too young to understand it all, he had known one thing—love meant making yourself vulnerable. Love meant pain. And he would never do that to himself willingly.

He tipped his head back and took a long swallow of the brandy. The lights from the park cast an otherworldly glow over the high rises that soared behind it. It was as mystifying a view of New York as his behavior had been tonight. Because even if he had been wrong about Olivia, even if Giovanni *had* been mentoring her as a way to pay back what he owed to her mother, even if she *was* that vulnerable, frightened creature he'd witnessed tonight that his grandfather had elected to shelter and protect, it didn't change anything. What he and Olivia had was a business deal. He was no white knight to ride in on a steed and save the day.

He finished off the brandy and set the glass down. Whatever crazy thing drew him to Olivia, whatever it had been between them from the start, was precisely what he needed to avoid. His only interest should be preserving his family legacy. In doing what had always been paramount for him. Allowing himself to care for anything beyond that had never been in the cards.

CHAPTER SEVEN

A WEEK INTO his and Olivia's return to Milan, every aspect of Rocco's plan seemed to be falling into perfect strategic place. The announcement of his fiancée as the new face of Mondelli was making waves across fashion circles, her sudden return to modeling an angle it seemed no media outlet could resist. And although some media chose to speculate on the reason behind Olivia's disappearance from modeling, most were universally positive about the union, choosing, as Savanna had predicted, to focus on the glamorous engagement of two high-profile personalities and brands rather than speculate on a story for which they had no answers.

He glanced down at the front page of the weekly gossip magazine that typically featured royalty on the cover, but instead this week featured *the kiss*, as the press had dubbed it. The one he and Olivia had shared at the press conference.

He'd seen more of the vivid, easy smile on Olivia's face the tabloid had featured in the after shot since they'd returned to Milan, his fiancée seeming to relax as soon as they'd cleared New York airspace. The staff at Villa Mondelli appeared to love her, and she seemed at peace roaming the beautiful grounds. It was only at night when they retired to the master suite that the tension ratcheted up between them. He'd taken to going to bed even later than he normally did, working in his office until he was sure Olivia was asleep. Because to do otherwise was asking for trouble.

He took the last sip of his espresso and pushed the cup away. His efforts to harness his potent attraction toward his pretend fiancée had been successful. If he didn't see, touch or hear her, he was okay. And he intended to keep it that way. Particularly when he was now sure he'd been right. His grandfather would never have had a relationship with her. He must have been out of his head to think it possible.

The knowledge removed a barrier he instead needed to be ten times thicker.

Gabriella stuck her head in his office. "You need to leave now if you're going to make it to your lunch."

His mouth curved. "Even with my driving?"

"Even with your driving," she acknowledged drily.

"On my way."

His nemesis was seated at a prime table near the windows when Rocco entered the popular seafood restaurant, the chairman's quick glance at his watch as he sat down indicating he was five minutes late. Rocco didn't bother to acknowledge it. Rialto pointed at his glass. "I've ordered a bottle of merlot. I thought we could toast your very successful week."

A satisfied rush blanketed him. "I thought it so."

"Landing Olivia Fitzgerald as a face and a wife? I almost feel you've taken my advice to heart. Although I am surprised given your thoughts on the matter the last time we spoke."

"I've reconsidered." Rocco waited while the *cameriera* uncorked then served their wine, before fixing Renzo with an even look. "You wanted me to think about what is best for Mondelli. I have."

"It's the speed with which you have done so that worries me," the chairman said drily. "This is not a chess match, Rocco. This is the future of the company your grandfather built. When we spoke last time about witnessing some long-term stability with you, I was asking for a true commitment, not smoke and mirrors."

Rocco's blood heated to a dangerous level. "You forget it was *I* who quadrupled the market value of Mondelli. I *do* have this company's best interests at heart. Which is why I have executed a strategic merger that is pure brilliance."

Renzo eyed him. "Olivia Fitzgerald is undeniably breathtaking, and I'm sure provides a wealth of distraction in the bedroom, but not necessarily what I intended when I suggested marriage. She is unpredictable given her recent past. A wild child."

"It is a perfect union from every angle," Rocco countered flatly. "A dynasty of two great brands."

Renzo took a long, deliberate sip of his wine, set his glass down and sat back, arms folded across his chest. "You don't see it, do you?"

"See what?"

"The Mondelli men's weakness when it comes to women. *Pensare con quello che hai in mezzo alle gambe al posto della testa...*"

Thinking with what's between your legs and not your head... Rocco ground his back teeth together. "That…"

Renzo waved a hand at him. "Giovanni made a fool out of himself over Tatum Fitzgerald. He forgot his priorities, let his head get swelled by having her even though he was a happily married man, and the company stuttered. Your father's career imploded over the love of a woman." He shook his head. "Make a smart decision, Rocco, not one in which you're thumbing your nose at all of us."

Blood thudded through his head in a deafening rush. He leaned forward, rested his elbows on the table and met the chairman's gaze. "I am not my father, nor my grandfather, Renzo. I am the man who took a struggling company and raised it to a higher level. You *need* me. Don't forget that important fact."

"And you need me," Renzo countered deliberately. "You have taken Mondelli to great heights, Rocco. No one can dispute that. I'm simply giving you some advice."

Rocco sat back in his seat. "So you have. Are we done on this subject?"

"Set a date."

Rocco frowned. *"Mi scusi?"*

"If you want to convince the board you are truly a changed man, set a wedding date."

The blood thumping against his temples converged in a pool of disbelief. "You're joking?"

Renzo's mouth twisted. "It is my job to ensure control is turned over to you when you are well and truly ready. *I* am responsible to the shareholders, and in this day and age, perception is as important as reality. *They* think you are a question mark, Rocco—unpredictable at best. So if Olivia Fitzgerald is the choice, marry her. Show your intentions."

Rocco thought he must be hallucinating. "Olivia and I are far too busy to plan a wedding right now."

"Undoubtedly." Renzo's gaze narrowed on him. "But I suggest you do it. The sooner you prove to the board you can run Mondelli with the measured, mature perspective of a man who's sown his wild oats, the quicker we will be to hand over control."

Rocco absorbed the unyielding glint in the chairman's eyes. "You are *actually* telling me to speed up my wedding date to pacify shareholder perception?"

The older man's eyes glittered back at him with something like unmediated glee. "We all sacrifice things, Rocco. I don't love my wife. I married her because she was the perfect partner for a CEO. Power comes with sacrifice, and if you don't realize that by now, you will learn."

He bit back the response that rose in his throat. He didn't

have to explain to Renzo he'd known sacrifice since he was a teenager bringing up his baby sister. Since he'd been fresh out of school, deep in over his head, running a company so vast he'd lain awake at night in the early days, his mind reeling on how to corral it. How to fix it.

He picked up his wine and took a long sip. It was a bitter pill to swallow, but Renzo was right. At the end of the day what mattered was what the analysts said about him. And they thought he was a maverick.

He'd never intended on marrying for love—so why *not* marry Olivia? It didn't do anything but cement the plan he'd already put into place.

His hand tightened around the glass as he set it down. Renzo was also right about Olivia. He might think he was in control, but she was a danger to him. He *had* thought and acted with what was between his legs and not his head. Just like Giovanni had done.

He would not repeat history. He would not be that weak.

Olivia was chatting over some designs with a gregarious Mario Masini when her fiancé deigned to make an appearance in the design studios. He had pretty much disappeared since they'd returned home from New York, thrown himself into his ridiculous fourteen-hour days and communicated with the short verbiage of a man too busy to converse when they eventually sat down at the dinner table together at the villa.

She was aware he was deliberately putting space between them after their close encounters in New York, and she got it. She was glad for it. So why did she feel barefoot and rejected? Because for *one* second there, a voice in her head jibed, she'd thought he actually cared. Some delusional part of her brain had conjured that up. When what she really was was an asset to be managed. That was all.

Mario moved to embrace Rocco, his lined old face softening. Her fiancé was drool worthy again today in a silver gray suit and blue tie that never seemed to wrinkle. Elegant and earthy all at the same time, he was a man with so much sex appeal he was drowning in it.

"Ciao," she murmured as casually as she could, waving a hand to the designs spread out on the table. "Mario and I were just chatting over fabrics. Is it that time already?"

His mouth curved. "Thirty minutes past. It isn't a problem. We're eating in tonight. Take your time."

She almost wished they were staying at Villa Mondelli, where she could put a literal and figurative distance between them at the formal dining room table. Instead, they were staying at the apartment so she could make her 7:00 a.m. photo shoot with Alessandra tomorrow without getting up obscenely early.

Mario pointed at the designs on the table. "She is brilliant, this woman of yours. It's as if she brings the light inside with her."

Rocco nodded. "That's a very apt description."

Mario smiled broadly. "We are going to make her a star of the design world."

Olivia's heart swelled. Instead of accepting her warily into the fold, Mario had seemed incredibly enthusiastic over her designs, as if he, too, welcomed the infusion of creativity as Giovanni had.

She couldn't help the smile that stretched her lips. It was happening. Her dream was actually happening.

Rocco flicked a look at her. "Do what you need to do. I'll answer some emails."

But he didn't. She tried to concentrate on her conversation with Mario, but with Rocco roaming the room, pulling her pieces off the rack, flicking sketches apart and staring at them with that trademark intensity of his, she was hopelessly distracted. A few minutes later, Mario made an amused comment about her attention span and "young lovers" and announced they were done for the day.

Rocco waited until the older man had left the studio before his gaze slid over her face. "Either your acting skills have kicked in, or my presence is making you nervous."

She lifted her chin. "You're looking at my designs properly for the first time. My future rests in your hands... Wouldn't you expect me to be heart in mouth?"

His mouth twisted. "I thought that was just the general effect I had on you, *bella*."

She rested her hands on her hips. "I'm not the one working until 1:00 a.m. to avoid being in a bedroom together. Are your control-freak tendencies on red alert?"

His ebony gaze darkened. "As a matter of fact, they are. Your little stunt in New York wasn't exactly a cure for a man practicing abstinence. Nor is the provocative way you sleep splayed across my bed." He shrugged an elegant shoulder. "I keep thinking maybe it's just easier to get it over with. How simple it would be to slide a hand under the small of your back, tempt you with what I know you've been dying to have, then take you long and hard until all you'd be doing is *begging* me to come to bed. *Then* maybe we could snuff this out."

Her insides dissolved into a river of fire, his taunt sending the intimate flesh at the heart of her into an excited, heated pull. She could not believe he'd just said that.

A hard glitter entered his eyes. "But of course, that will never happen."

She sank her teeth into her bottom lip as her brain crashed rapidly back to earth. Turning, she stacked the designs on the table into neat piles, anger pulsing through her. "Oh, I get it, Rocco. You won't put a hand on me because you think I was your grandfather's lover, that I am soiled goods. But you want to, so you use your shock value to send me running." She straightened the last pile, leaned back against the table and looked up at him. "Have I got it right?"

The in-your-face arrogance faded from his face. "I owe you an apology."

That caught her off guard. "For what?"

"For assuming things that were not true. I was angry and I made accusations I shouldn't have about your and Giovanni's relationship. But the facts were staring me in the face."

Antagonism replaced her confusion. "What facts? The fact he'd *loaned* me an apartment?"

"*Bought* it for you. The fact that he was writing you checks for large sums of money. That he never mentioned you at all. It was not normal behavior for Giovanni. Even your neighbors thought you were lovers."

"Because he would come visit me at night to work?" She sank her hands deeper into her hips and glared at him. "You assumed a great deal of things, Rocco, and you were dead wrong on all of them."

He inclined his head. "I was angry. Grieving. To accept that the Giovanni I knew would have cheated on Rosa, that he could be anything but the intensely loyal man I knew him to be, was exceedingly difficult."

Undoubtedly. Her mouth flattened. "It still didn't give you the right to treat me like you did."

His face tightened. "I am apologizing."

She'd bet he rarely, if ever, did it. It probably made him want to choke. But the relief flaring through her was undeniable. That finally he believed her. It had been like a palpable force between them, stirring mistrust on every level.

She eyed the conflicting emotions shimmering in his eyes. He needed to understand.

She crossed her arms over her chest and held his gaze. "Giovanni told me Rosa was his first love. That he couldn't imagine ever being with anyone else. Then he met my mother and he was blindsided. She did one of his break-through shows in New York. He was on a high from his success, higher than he'd ever been, and my mother was the glittering jewel he couldn't resist."

"He should have," Rocco growled.

"He knew that. He said being with her was like some inescapable force he couldn't resist. And he wondered if he'd married too early."

"Rosa was pregnant with my father at eighteen. They had no choice but to marry."

She nodded. "It was a very different kind of love he had with Rosa—the inviolate pureness of it. What he felt for my mother was passionate, intense. And he was torn."

"Because he was *married*," he ground out, eyes flashing. "Because my grandmother *lived for him*."

Her heart constricted. "Giovanni seemed like some mystical force, but he was human, just like we all are. I get how you feel, I do. I watched my father fall apart because his wife was in love with someone else. I *lived* through it. I hated my mother for my entire teenage years for doing that to us. I still hate her a bit for it. And I wanted to hate Giovanni, too… But when he explained how it was between them, I finally got it. It was never about them deliberately trying to hurt other people. It was about feelings beyond their control."

His lip curled. "A lovely reiteration of a modern-day Romeo and Juliet story, Liv. Believe me, I do get it—the idea of temptation, how that temptation, that depth of love, can destroy everything around you. It is my father's life. It's why I go to such lengths to never let it rule me. It's a weak man's poison."

She frowned. "Giovanni was not weak."

"I don't know what he was anymore." The admission was torn from him in a low, gravelly tone. "But I know he couldn't have been your lover. That was me projecting my anger onto you."

She expelled a long breath.

"Who ended it, then?" he asked abruptly. "How did he choose?"

"Rosa. She found out about the affair, told Giovanni he had to choose and, when he did, forbade him ever to see my mother again."

"It was never in his head to go back to your mother once Rosa died?"

A poignant smile twisted her mouth. "I asked him that. He said once you travel through some doors, you can never go back."

He was quiet for a long time. Then he walked over to the racks where her designs hung and pulled a couple out. "Mario is right. You are insanely talented."

For a moment she actually didn't know what to say. "Thank you," she said finally.

He came back to lean against the table beside her. "There is a change we have to make in the deal."

Her heart stuttered. Being so close to her dream and having it be plucked away from her would kill her.

"I met with the chairman of the board today. There is a general sentiment among the board and shareholders that I am a wild card in the wake of Giovanni's death. My tendency to want to do things my way ruffles feathers. My bachelor persona fails to keep those invested in the company tucked securely in their beds at night with sweet dreams of dollar figures running through their heads. They want to see me stable. Married."

A flicker of unease slanted through her. This made the reasons for their engagement clear. Given the Columbia Four's rather wild reputation, she could understand why the board might be uneasy with such a young, strong-minded CEO.

"We just announced our engagement," she said haltingly. "How much more could they want?"

A cynical smile twisted his lips. "They want a date. A marriage."

Her knees went weak. "As in us walking down the aisle?"

"Exactly like that, *cara*." She didn't like the premeditated look that stretched his olive-skinned face as he turned the full force of his will on her. "Nothing changes, except we tie the knot in six weeks. Our one-year agreement is still in place and Mondelli brings your designs to market just as we said."

"Six weeks?" The words came out as a high-pitched squeak.

He shrugged. "You told me yourself you never planned to get married. A quick, uncontested divorce with all the terms outlined will be painless."

Painless? Her fingers caught the side of the table in a death grip. So this was why he'd been softening her up. Complimenting her designs…

She shook her head. "Oh, no. You are not bullying me into this, Rocco. I am not walking down the aisle with you, lying to the world in six weeks. It's too much."

"Ah, but you are, sweet Liv." The smile that curved his lips was far from reassuring. "It's inconvenient, I agree. The last thing either of us needs to be doing right now is planning a wedding. But it is what it is. And we both continue to get what we want."

The media circus of last week's press conference flashed through her head. The horrible, paralyzing, *naked* feeling of being in the spotlight again. Her stomach swirled with nausea at the thought of it—*ten times worse.*

"You are out of your mind," she breathed. "Tell the board I won't hurry my wedding for them. Tell them whatever you like. But this is *not happening.*"

This time he wasn't getting his way.

CHAPTER EIGHT

FASHION PHOTOGRAPHERS WEREN'T known to be the most subtle of breeds. The ones Olivia had worked with in the past had ranged from sophisticated persuaders, like her former lover Guillermo, to the completely indifferent, to full-out beasts who yelled at you and told you you had half the talent the last model had.

In this regard, Alessandra was a breed apart. She was incredibly patient, encouraging and had an amazing eye for the composition of a great shot. Unfortunately for the talented young photographer, Olivia hadn't given her anything to work with over the morning, and they both knew it. She was stiff, awkward and without her usual grace, struggling to find her groove.

Close to lunchtime, Alessandra finally pulled her camera over her head and set it on a table. "Let's take a break," she suggested. "We'll start again in fifteen."

Come back when you're able to give me something to work with. Alessandra didn't say it, but her eyes did. Olivia's shoulders sagged. The shot Alessandra wanted for the fall/winter catalog was one of her leaning on a fence in a fabulous crepe dress, reeking of dreamy impatience as she waited for her lover to pick her up.

The mood just wouldn't come. Maybe because the last kiss she and Rocco had shared was that almost one in the New York apartment when she'd nearly made a fool out of herself over him. Again.

Not inspirational.

"I'm assuming my brother has something to do with the shadows under your eyes," Alessandra guessed mischievously. "For any number of reasons."

True, but not when it came to the wild romps in the sack Alessandra was undoubtedly referring to. Rocco's outrageous suggestion they get married had kept her awake until the early hours of the morning.

She frowned. "Is he always such a browbeating autocrat?"

Alessandra laughed. "A well-meaning one, yes. He gets what he wants."

"He *wants* us to get married in six weeks."

"Six weeks?" Alessandra looked horrified. "Why so soon?"

"The board is asking us to speed up our wedding. They want to see Rocco married before they put their full confidence behind him."

Rocco's sister pursed her lips. "I guess it makes sense given Giovanni didn't leave him a controlling stake in Mondelli. Rocco's bachelor behavior has always antagonized the board, but without a controlling stake, they can dictate what they like and tie his hands." Her gaze turned sympathetic. "Not that *you* should have to speed up your wedding because of it."

Olivia's mouth dropped open. "Mondelli is your family's business. How could Giovanni not have left Rocco a controlling stake?"

"Giovanni put Renzo Rialto, the chairman of the board, in charge of the controlling ten percent of Mondelli to give Rocco some time to find his feet without him. My brother is brilliant and responsible for building Mondelli into a global powerhouse, but Giovanni was always there to keep him in check."

Olivia rocked back on her heels. It all made sense now.

Why Rocco hadn't told the board to go to hell with its demands. Because he couldn't.

She shook the haze out of her head. "I think I'll get that air."

Rocco told himself he wasn't checking up on Olivia, but he knew he was. She'd been so tight-lipped and unapproachable this morning, he actually wondered if she was going to refuse to marry him. And since that couldn't happen, since Mondelli's fall/winter Vivo campaign for which Alessandra was shooting today was worth ten million dollars, here he was at her shoot when he should be going over the monthly numbers with the CFO.

Alessandra gave him a warm hug. "Couldn't stay away?"

"You could put it that way. How is she doing?"

"She's been a bit of a stiff mess." She frowned up at him. "That isn't the same woman I shot two years ago, Rocco. What happened to her?"

He lifted a shoulder. "She won't talk about it. To anyone. I have tried, believe me."

"Can you go talk to her? Nothing we've taken this morning is going to work. If this continues, it's going to be a total waste of a day."

He nodded and made his way out onto the terrace, where Olivia was standing at the railing staring down at the courtyard below. She looked like an exotic bird perched for flight.

The guilt inside him ratcheted a layer deeper. *Per l'amor di Dio.* He did not need to be walking around with a living, breathing case of remorse. They were both getting what they needed out of this.

He joined her at the railing. Surprise wrote its way across her beautiful face. "I thought you had a packed day."

"I wanted to check on you. You seemed off this morning."

She turned to face him, blue eyes flashing. "You are railroading me into marrying you. You are asking me to stand in front of a priest and *lie* about my feelings for you. Forgive me if I think this is taking things a bit far."

He inclined his head. "I agree that part isn't easy. But it's necessary."

"Necessary for *you*." She crossed her arms over her chest. "You are right about my dream, Rocco. I want it badly. Badly enough to marry you. With one condition."

He lifted a brow.

"I want my own line. My own signature line at Mondelli. *I* want to control my destiny."

He frowned. "Mario has to okay those decisions."

"Then get him to. Or find yourself another fiancée."

He studied her for a long moment. Read her determination. "All right," he said quietly. "I'm sure we can come to some agreement. Anything else bothering you?"

Her mouth twisted wryly. "Alessandra told you I was a disaster."

"Not a disaster. Just not yourself."

She turned and looked out at the rooftops. "I'm afraid I've lost my touch. That I don't have it anymore. It used to come so easily to me, and this morning was…a disaster."

"Olivia." He slid a hand around her waist and turned her to him. "Whatever happened to you a year ago, whatever it is you won't talk about, *is* ancient history. Go in there and be the model you are. I guarantee you will be jaw-dropping."

Her brilliant blue eyes darkened into a deep, azure blue. "What if I can't?" she asked huskily. "What if I can't get it back and you've wasted five million dollars on me?"

He shook his head. "You don't lose that kind of talent. What you're fighting is in your head."

Doubt flickered in her eyes, her gaze dropping away from his. He slid his fingers under her chin and made her look up at him. "You know I'm right."

"What would you know about it?" she asked tartly. "You've probably never had an unsure day in your life."

"That's where you're wrong, *cara*. When I was young, when I first took over as CEO of Mondelli, I thought I had it all figured out. I spearheaded this big deal, overrode Giovanni's protests that it wasn't right for the company and brought us close to bankruptcy."

Her eyes widened. "And you know what Giovanni said to me? He didn't berate me. He didn't say, 'I told you so.' He told me to learn from my mistake. To never make the same one again." He shrugged, a wry smile twisting his mouth. "It rocked me, to be sure. For months I was wary, afraid to take any big steps, but eventually I learned to trust my judgment again. To trust my instincts. And so will you."

She blinked. "You really almost bankrupted Mondelli?"

"Sì." He gave her a reprimanding look. "So go back in there, relax and figure it out. You haven't lost your talent, it's just lying dormant."

He thought he saw some level of understanding in her eyes. But she was too tense, too stiff, to ever make this work, and it *had* to work. Ignoring his better judgment, he slid his palms down over her hips to cup her derriere, pulling her flush against him. Her eyes flew wide. "What are you doing?"

"Solving this problem the only way I know how."

She was midway through a reply when he claimed her lips. Their sweet softness under his sent all his good sense out the window. Turned what had been a deliberate quest to loosen her up into a seduction of himself instead. His body seemed to be programmed with a particular weakness for her. For the taste of her. For how she felt under his hands…

And his thirst for her consumed him. He wanted what he couldn't have so badly it was like a fever in his blood.

He slid his hands into the weight of her silky hair and took what he wanted. She responded this time, as if she couldn't fight it any more than he could. An animal sense of satisfaction rumbled through him as he imprinted her with the need that had been consuming him for weeks. The soft contours of her body melted into his, invited him closer. He closed his fingers tighter around a mass of satiny hair and arched her head back to deepen the kiss. To stake complete ownership.

Her lips parted beneath his, an invitation he couldn't ignore. He dipped his tongue into the heat of her. Her taste mingled with his, the absolute perfection of what they created together rocking him to his toes.

That night in Navigli hadn't been an aberration. It had been a foregone conclusion.

He ran his hands down her back, sought out any remaining tension with the sweep of his fingers, kneaded a knot free with a press of his thumbs.

A discreet cough came from behind them. They whirled around in unison to find Alessandra had joined them on the terrace, an amused look plastered across her face. "Sorry, you two, but we need to get started."

Olivia nodded jerkily, wiping her palm across her mouth. Alessandra went back inside.

"I can't believe I just did that," Olivia said, staring at the lipstick on her palm. "Which point were you trying to prove this time, Rocco? That you are irresistible now that the spoiled-goods sign has been lifted from me?"

Anger at himself, at her, welled up inside of him. "Actually, Liv," he muttered, "I was trying to comfort you. To be there for you. Like it or not, we are in this together."

Color bled into her cheeks. "A team? I seem to remember you proclaiming me a purchased asset."

He raked a hand through his hair. "I might have been a bit overbearing. We are marrying now. It would be nice if we can be there for each other. Call a truce to this war of ours."

She shook her head. "Forgive me if it's not so easy for me to process your one-hundred-and-eighty-degree turns."

The bustling movements of the crew moving around inside captured his attention. "They need you in there," he advised roughly. "Go channel how much you hate me. You'll do just fine."

She studied him warily for a moment, then walked back inside. He stayed at the railing. What was wrong with him? He had to stay away from her. But something about Olivia, something about who she was inside, how vulnerable she was, seemed to waltz right past his defenses every time.

And wasn't that *insane*? He felt like finding a mirror and double-checking this was still him. Because wasn't it enough to know Tatum Fitzgerald had torn his steadfast, larger-than-life grandfather in two? Did he even have to question what allowing himself to feel emotion for Olivia would do to him?

He had told himself not to cross the line. Not to let himself feel. Yet he had just crossed so far over the line he couldn't pretend not to be emotionally involved anymore.

He swore and pushed away from the railing. That absolutely, positively could not happen. Not when Renzo Rialto and the board wanted to eat him alive, and that was the only place his focus should be.

He strode back inside, avoiding the controlled chaos on the set as he headed toward the elevators. He was shutting this thing with Olivia down. Finding another strategy, because this one obviously wasn't working.

Olivia watched Rocco disappear into the elevator, her equilibrium smashed to pieces. She had no idea what had just happened. Was Rocco just as confused about his feelings for her as she was of hers for him, or was he just using her again? She was tempted to think he really did care, that what she'd sensed that night in New York was real. But that was dangerous thinking for a woman about to marry him for show. For a woman he was clearly using to regain control of his company.

As for him suddenly asserting they were a team in this? She shook her head as she sank down in the makeup chair. That would be a foolish, *foolish* thing to believe.

But as she walked back onto the set after her makeup had been repaired, she couldn't help but remember what Rocco had said. She *had* once been phenomenal at this. At creating an illusion. It *was* all in her head. She just had to bear down and do it.

She would never have admitted it, but when Alessandra tried again with that pose of her leaning against a fence with her baby finger in her mouth, the heat from Rocco's kiss filled her head. And she wondered what would happen if she were ever stupid enough to let him take her to bed.

Complete and total annihilation.

When Alessandra finally put her camera down and announced them finished, Olivia gave her an apprehensive look. "Did you get everything you needed?"

Alessandra quirked a finger at her. "These five shots are worth the day."

They were, of course, the photos of her leaning against the fence, her finger dangling innocently from her mouth, Rocco's stamp written all over her. The look on her face stole the breath from her throat.

"Exactly," Alessandra said with satisfaction. "You look utterly, delectably, madly in love."

CHAPTER NINE

NEW YORK DURING Fashion Week was a frenetic exercise in seeing and being seen. Anyone who was anyone in the fashion world descended on the city like a swarm of locusts ready to make their mark. Press coverage was massive, celebrity sightings in an already star-encrusted city even more frequent and thousand-dollar bottles of Cristal ran like water in the dozens of warm-up parties held across the metropolis.

There was, however, no partying going on at the Mondelli suite at Fifteen Central Park West on the afternoon of the Italian fashion house's show, Olivia's first appearance on a runway in over twelve months. The show, combined with the details of planning the society wedding of the year, had Olivia hurtling close to the edge. She was wearing the face of Medusa. Rocco was afraid if he touched her, she would snap in half.

She stood, hands on jean-clad hips, in the salon, blue eyes shooting fire at him. "I told you I don't care," she muttered in response to his question about the wedding color scheme. "Maybe we should make it a black-and-white theme—the light and the darkness."

"Perfetto," he murmured. "You would be the darkness and I would be the light."

"As if." She shoved the guest list back at him. "I told you. Violetta, Sophia, my mother and my father. That's it. And my father is not walking me down the aisle."

"Why?"

"Because he has his own family now, and who knows if he'll be able to take the time off work. He works long hours for the transit company."

Rocco frowned. "So I'll send him some money to cover the week. Maybe he and his family can even make a vacation out of it."

"You will not." Heat flared in her eyes. "He hasn't wanted anything to do with my mother and me for years. Leave him alone."

"Let's talk about your mother, then. If you've forgiven Giovanni and her for the affair, why the animosity?"

"Forgiving her for the affair has nothing to do with my general feelings for my mother."

"Which are?" He lifted a brow. "I'm going to be meeting her tonight. Maybe you should give me a heads-up as to what I'm walking into."

"Like you did with Stefan?" She shook her still-damp hair back over her shoulders. "All she cares about is status. Keeping up with the Joneses."

He frowned. "It must have been hard for her when her career fell apart. When she lost Giovanni and your father."

"She brought it on herself. And then she made everyone pay." Olivia got down on her hands and knees and peered under the coffee table. "Have you seen my sneakers? We have to be out of here in five minutes."

He shook his head and shrugged on his jacket. "What do you mean 'made everyone pay'?"

"Dammit, I need those sneakers." She crawled over and looked under the sofa. "They're my lucky ones. Are you sure you haven't seen them?"

Rocco walked to the door, found her sneakers jammed under a pair of his dress shoes and fished them out. He carried them over to her but held them out of reach.

"Tell me."

She got to her feet and grabbed the running shoes out of his hands. "When I began to have success with modeling, my mother latched on to me as if I was her saving grace. Her career was done, and she had a hard time holding a normal job. So she spent my money like it was cheap wine. Went on living her life like she had in the good old days. The more she spent, the more I had to work to pay the bills. I was exhausted, in a different city every week. But it never stopped. It was an endless vicious cycle of wanting to cut back and not being able to."

His brows came together. "Are you saying she spent all your money?"

She sat down and tugged a shoe on. "I'm saying that when I returned home from a trip to Europe where my credit card was declined, the bank manager told me I was broke. As in *zero* dollars in the bank. She had spent it all."

His stomach lurched. "On what? What could she have spent that much money on?"

She yanked the other shoe on. "An apartment, a car, trips to visit her friends in the south of France. I was so busy working I had no idea."

"And you trusted her," he concluded grimly.

"Who would you trust more with your life than your mother?"

Or your father. The uneasy feeling in his stomach intensified. The way he had read this woman wrong from the very beginning on every point shamed him to his core. She hadn't been out partying away her money. She had been attempting to support her family, just as he had had to.

"Mi dispiace," he said quietly as she stood there, a vulnerability emanating from her he now knew to be utterly authentic. "I have judged you completely wrong from the beginning, Olivia. I owe you an apology."

She stared back at him for a long moment, surprise

etching its way across her face. Self-disgust kicked in his gut. He had really been a first-class ass this entire time.

Her gaze fell away from his. "We should go. I need to be backstage in half an hour."

Olivia tried to ignore the seismic shift that seemed to have occurred in her and Rocco's relationship as they walked the short distance to the Lincoln Center. It had been there ever since that kiss during the photo shoot. Ever since he'd told her he believed her about her and Giovanni's relationship. He may have been avoiding her even more the past couple of weeks, but he was different with her. His respect for her showed. He'd stopped treating her like a high-priced show horse he'd purchased, his to bend to his will.

Rocco came backstage with her to greet the designers and models. Frederic, who was producing the show, gave her a hug and a kiss on the cheek. "Put that face away," he scolded. "You are going to shine tonight. They can't wait to see you."

That made her stomach squeeze into an even tighter ball.

"By the way," Frederic said quietly as models and crew members flowed past them, "Guillermo is shooting backstage tonight."

"Oh." She caught her lip between her teeth and considered that. She hadn't seen Guillermo since the night she had walked out on him, her own heart broken in two. "Thanks for the heads-up," she said huskily. "How is he?"

"Fine. Single. Here any minute." He gave her an affectionate push toward the makeup room. "They're ready for you."

She was made up, desperately trying to distract herself from the way the mood had shifted backstage from one of industrious, purposeful action to an electric, anticipatory tension that sizzled in her veins, when a familiar voice rang out. She turned around and saw her designer-clad mother making her way toward her with Rocco in tow. *Great.*

She rose and gave her an awkward hug. "I thought we were going to meet at the reception afterward?"

"And wait to meet your delicious fiancé?" Her mother wrinkled her nose. "You're on the runway again, sweetie. It's so fabulous. I wanted to come and wish you good luck."

"That's very sweet of you. But would you mind giving me some space before the show?"

Her mother peered at her. "Are you okay, hon? You look nervous."

She *was* nervous. She wanted to throw up. She wanted to put her clothes back on, run out of here and never come back.

Rocco curved a hand around her mother's shoulder. "Why don't I show you to the seat beside mine and we can all catch up after the show?"

Her mother beamed. "That sounds wonderful."

Olivia almost loved him in that moment. Almost.

Tanya, one of the designers, appeared with her first outfit, an ultrachic emerald-green cocktail dress. Olivia shrugged out of her robe and slid it over her head, every movement mechanical, born of years of practice. Tanya fussed around her for a few minutes, making sure the dress fell perfectly, then pronounced her ready.

She walked out into the wings, joining the other models clustered there, her pounding heart a raging contrast to the ice in her limbs. *You can do this*, she told herself. *You can.*

"Livvie." Guillermo materialized in front of her, two cameras slung around his neck. He was as dark and devilishly handsome as ever, his swarthy skin a perfect foil for his amazing green eyes. He drank her in, gaze full of affection. "You look incredible."

"Gui." She stepped forward and pressed a kiss to both his cheeks. "It's so good to see you. How have you been?"

His smile was wry. "Since I've recovered from your heart smashing and disappearance? I was worried about you, Liv. You could at least have let me know you were okay."

She bit her lip. "I thought maybe a clean break was better for us."

A flicker of something she knew she had put there glimmered in his eyes. "Maybe so." He frowned. "Do you think we could talk afterward? I know you're engaged to Mondelli, it's not that. I just want to make sure you're okay."

Her teeth sank deeper into her lip. She was starting to realize what it was like to be hopelessly besotted with someone and not have those feelings returned. "Gui..."

A flash of platinum blond flew past her. She turned and stared at the model joining the line, her wildly excited expression marking her new in the business. Something contracted deep inside of Olivia at the sight of the young girl's pert nose and ridiculously high cheekbones.

Petra. But Petra was dead...

The bottle of water she held slipped from her fingers and fell to the floor.

Guillermo picked it up. "It's Natasha," he murmured quietly. "Petra's sister."

The image of Petra's vibrant young sister, an almost identical younger version of her friend, giggling with the other models, collided with Olivia's last memory of her best friend. Petra had been lying prone across her living room sofa, her face chalk white, her expressive eyes vacant. Olivia's fingers had stumbled over the keys of her phone, desperately dialing 9-1-1. But it had been too late.

She wasn't aware the wounded, animallike sound had come from her until Guillermo reached for her arm, an alarmed expression on his face. "Liv..."

"No." She shook him off and started walking. Anywhere but here, looking at *that.* She was dimly aware of Frederic announcing it was ten minutes to showtime.

She kept walking past him. His eyes widened and he followed her.

"Liv." He tugged on her arm. "What the hell are you doing? You're starting the show."

She broke free and kept walking. "I'm sorry. I can't. I just…can't."

In the back of the wings, she sat down in a chair and put her head between her legs. The frantic sounds of a show about to happen filled her ears. Haunted her with her biggest failure… She put her fingers to her temples as the world swirled around her, darker and darker. Beckoned her with its beguiling promise of escape. She'd thought she was strong enough to do this. But she wasn't.

"Liv." Rocco's voice penetrated the darkness. "What's wrong?"

She shook her head. Shook him away.

He knelt down in front of her and captured her jaw in his hands. "Look at me."

She shook him off. "Go away."

"Nessuno." He captured her jaw again, this time tighter, his fingers digging into her flesh. "I will not allow you to destroy yourself like this. Tell me what's wrong."

She wrenched herself free. *"I can't do this.* My best friend overdosed after she walked off this stage, Rocco. Because she couldn't handle the pressure anymore. It's why I left. *I can't do it."*

His eyes widened. "I'm so sorry. I had no idea."

A lone tear broke through the wall she had built around herself. "I loved her. She was my rock. She was the *strong* one. And *I* allowed that to happen to her."

"You didn't *allow* anything," he countered roughly. "She was suffering, Olivia. That type of suffering requires professional attention. You couldn't have stopped it."

She squeezed her eyes shut. "I can't go out there. Tell Frederic to replace me."

"Yes, you can. *Look at me, damn you.*" She kept her eyes squeezed tightly shut. He took hold of her shoulders and shook her. *"Look at me."*

She opened her eyes. His gaze held hers. "All that is out there is a walk, Liv. A walk down a runway. *It* doesn't define you. Your extraordinary talent does. And if you don't go out there tonight, if you turn your back on all those people, you are alienating everyone who matters. Everyone who will decide whether those beautiful designs you and Giovanni created together will touch the world." His expression softened, dark and sure. "And they will touch the world because they are genius, *cara. You* are a genius. But you have to let them see it."

Another tear burned a hot track down her cheek. "You don't have to say that."

"Do I ever say anything I don't mean?" He pressed his forehead against hers. "Make this the night you leave the darkness behind. Because you are light, Olivia. Everything about you is radiant. Don't let them win."

The tears fell harder. She wanted to. She wanted to let them win. She had already done that when she'd left the first time. But her dream hadn't been on the line then...

The pounding music and the MC's voice as he opened the show made her blood turn to ice. She drew back and stared blindly at Rocco. "I can't."

"Yes, you can." The quiet conviction in his eyes held her, wound its way around her insides. "Just you walking down a runway, Liv. That's all this is. Nothing more. You've done it hundreds of times. Let's do it together."

She swallowed hard. Felt his words penetrate the numbness. If she walked now, she *was* giving up everything. Everything she had created with Giovanni. Her reputation could only take so many knocks.

"Four passes," Rocco promised. "Four passes down that catwalk and you're done. Put it on automatic pilot and go."

She had to. She had to do it, she realized. For Giovanni. For herself.

"Okay." She swiped the tears from her cheeks. "Okay."

Frederic materialized. She stood, legs wobbly, Rocco's arm firm around her waist. The urge to hang on to him and never let go consumed her. He nodded at her, a smile curving his lips. "I'll be right here waiting for you."

Frederic swept her to the front of the line of models, but her cue had just come and went as the music pounded to life and general pandemonium ensued. She gave him a panicked look. "Forget it," he muttered, "go on the next line."

She focused on the long, light-encrusted runway rather than the crowd, sitting dozens of rows deep. The glare of the lights hit her as she walked onto the catwalk. She'd forgotten how hot they were, how long that thirty-six feet seemed when you were like a star in the sky…when all the attention was focused on you. The loud, pulsing beat of the music propelled her forward. Her walk wasn't her trademark cocky swagger, but it was steady and purposeful into the blinding light. She made it to the end of the runway, paused, stuck her hand into her hip and let the camera flashes reign down on her. Showed the dress off to its full advantage. The applause was deafening, but she blocked it out.

Just walking down a runway. That was all she was doing.

The three changes that came after, the brilliant showing that Mondelli and its new designers put in that night, it was all a blur. It wasn't until she did the final walk down the runway with the designers that she realized how weak her knees were. How close to collapsing she was. She shifted her weight, stood back, clapped for the designers and told herself to hold on for sixty more seconds.

After several standing ovations, they led the designers off the stage, Olivia willing herself through the curtain.

* * *

Rocco congratulated the designers as they came off the runway. The auditorium was abuzz, the evening triumphant, returning a resounding yes to the question many had posed as to whether Mondelli could survive without Giovanni. But his attention wasn't on the buzz; his eyes were locked on the curtain for Olivia.

She appeared, the rest of the models spilling through after her. The way her body slumped the minute she was through sent alarm slicing through him. She blinked to adjust to the light after the glare of the catwalk and scanned the wings. Searching for something. *Someone.*

A wave of protectiveness flashed through him. A smile curved his lips, his heart throbbing at her bravery. He was so proud of her, *so damn proud.*

Guillermo Villanueva stepped in front of him. He held his arms out to Olivia, and when she walked toward him, Rocco's heart stopped in his chest. Her name sprang to his lips, but he savagely stuffed it back in. His body tightened as he braced himself to watch Olivia walk into her former lover's arms. Then he realized she wasn't looking at Villanueva, she was looking past him. At *him.* Their gazes collided, the way Olivia's face fell apart as they did destroying something inside of him.

Villanueva turned around, focused on Rocco. A grimace twisted his lips as his arms fell to his sides. Rocco ignored him and moved toward Olivia. Her last shaky steps carried her into his arms. Her delicate floral scent enveloped him as he folded her against his chest.

"Sei stata magnifica," he murmured. "You were magnificent."

She stayed buried in his embrace for a long time. He was partially holding her up, but as the moments passed he felt the strength move back into her. When she finally pushed her palms against his chest and moved back, a tremulous smile curved her lips. "Just a walk down a runway," she whispered. "That's all it was."

He smiled. "That's all it was."

There were interviews to do, a reception to attend. Dinner he'd promised her mother. Olivia did the interviews with remarkable composure, following Savanna's instructions to gloss over any questions about missing her cue and put it down to backstage madness.

The desire not to leave her side, to anchor her, was unlike anything Rocco had ever felt before. It evoked a restless, uncomfortable feeling inside of him. As if for the first time in his life he had no idea what he was doing.

He smothered it, moved it aside. It had no place here. Not now.

Everyone at the reception, it seemed, wanted a piece of the return of Olivia Fitzgerald. And why wouldn't they? She was spectacular in the midnight blue gown that hugged every curve of her body and made her eyes glitter like the ocean on a particularly haunting night. Her hair plunged down her back in a swath of golden silk. But most powerful was the current that ran between them as he played guard dog and spirited Olivia through the necessary rounds. It stretched like a live force between them, cementing something both of them had known for weeks.

There was no escaping this.

They spent some time talking to Tatum Fitzgerald, whom Rocco found to be vain and narcissistic. So unlike Olivia it was almost impossible to believe they came from the same blood, except for their clearly matching outward genetics. He got them out of dinner with a promise to do so in Italy as Olivia's eyes begged for a reprieve. And then they were in the car being whisked through the warm Manhattan night.

CHAPTER TEN

THE APARTMENT WAS SILENT, bathed in the glow of the ever-present light of New York. After the pounding, pulsing rhythm of the night that had preceded it, the utter silence was like slamming on the brakes of his Aventador after he'd put the pedal to the floor. Full stop, jarring awareness. *Of everything.*

He threw his jacket over a chair, stripped his tie off and rolled up his sleeves. "Drink?" he asked Olivia, who was sitting on the sofa unbuckling her shoes.

She nodded.

He poured himself a much-needed tumbler of Scotch along with a glass of wine for her and crossed over to where Olivia stood at the windows.

"She was only twenty-five when she died." Her profile was ridiculously beautiful in the moonlight. "We met at a panty hose shoot when we were nineteen. They were asking us to say these ridiculous lines about how sexy the panty hose made us feel, and we both giggled our way through it. After that, we were best friends."

"You loved her a great deal."

She nodded. "She was the one who kept me sane. When there was too much money, too many people wanting to know us only because of who we were, too much partying and too much drinking. We were young and we had everything."

"But you didn't have everything."

"No." She turned to face him. "We were out of control near the end. I wasn't an alcoholic, but I was close. I always managed to rein myself in, but Petra couldn't. Her new boyfriend liked to do drugs, and it was a dangerous combination. I tried to get her to break up with him, but she was strong willed. One night—" her voice took on a gravelly note "—we were at a party and we split up. She went home with Ben and I stayed. A few hours later, I went to her apartment to check on her. But it was too late." A hot tear escaped the brimming pools of her eyes and slid down her cheek. "She was by herself and she didn't have a pulse."

His insides turned over. He captured her hand in his, wrapping his fingers tight around hers. "That must have been awful."

She looked down at the hand he held. "I was still holding her body when the paramedics told me she was dead. When they told me I had to let go."

"Mi dispiace." His voice was rough. "I am so very sorry, Olivia."

Her brilliant blue gaze clung to his. "If you hadn't been there tonight, I couldn't have done it. I would have destroyed myself."

He shook his head. "You would have walked out of there and you would have found your way."

"Not the right way." She pulled her hand free to swipe the tears from her face. Blinked hard. "I needed to face it. Face the past."

"And you did."

She nodded slowly as if just realizing that now. Her creamy skin was blotchy, her eyes red rimmed, but she was still the most bewitching woman he'd ever seen in his life and, with Olivia, it was not all on the outside. So much of what he hadn't seen in the beginning was inside that stunning exterior.

"Is that when the panic attacks started? When Petra died?"

She shook her head. "Those started when I was a teenager. My mother was emotionally unavailable, my father was gone, and there I was traveling to all these foreign countries under so much pressure." She looked out at the lights. "I went to see a therapist, learned how to try to control them, but they never went away. Sometimes they were worse than others."

"And that night in New York, that's what it was?"

"Yes." Her gaze stayed glued on the cityscape. "It was the end."

"Not the end," he countered softly. "You conquered it tonight."

"With you." She turned back to him, eyes brimming with emotion. "Thank you."

"That isn't necessary."

"Yes, it is. Rocco?"

"Sì?"

She brought her fingers to his lips. "Can we not talk anymore?"

Need roared to life inside of him, so fast and sharp it blinded him for a moment. He was in complete agreement, because to keep talking was rational, and *this* was not rational. He didn't want to think.

He captured her hand and pressed an intimate, openmouthed kiss against it. The way she tensed made his blood fire in his veins. "Do you still love him?"

She frowned. "Guillermo? I told you I never loved him the right way."

"Do you still *lust* after him, then?" He was shocked at how dark and gritty the words came out.

She looked down at the trembling hand he held in his. "What do you think?"

He put his drink down with a jerky movement. Took

hers and set it on the table beside his. Her gaze tracked him as he bent his head and allowed himself a mouthful of her bare, smooth shoulder. She was a silken, golden feast for him to explore, and she shuddered beneath his mouth. His stomach jammed into a tight, hard ball. Five weeks of wanting her had weakened him. Badly.

He blazed a path from her shoulder across the delicate skin of her collarbone to the throbbing pulse at the base of her neck. He was so enthralled with the taste of her, with the salty, sweet essence he had finally secured access to, he didn't hear her speak at first.

"Rocco?"

"Si?" He lifted his head and focused on her shimmering stare, glistening with the remnants of her tears.

"When did this become real?"

His heart stuttered in his chest, then stopped completely, his tongue unable to form the words.

Her gaze darkened. "I'm not asking for promises. I just need to know that *this*, tonight, whatever it is, it's real and not another of your games."

That he could answer. He lifted her palm and pressed it against the pounding beat of his heart, echoing her words. "What do you think?"

Her pupils dilated until they were dark glowing orbs in a sea of blue. She slid a hand behind his neck, tangled it in his hair and brought his mouth down to hers. He nipped at the lush fullness of her lower lip, teased her with tiny pulls that telegraphed his impatience. She was equally impatient, tugging on his hair and demanding his full attention. He consumed her then, taking her mouth in a series of hot, openmouthed kisses that made up for every last minute of these interminably long past few weeks. He kissed her until he'd explored every centimeter, every angle, of her, learned every mystery of her irresistible heart-shaped mouth. And then he demanded more, because his need for her was insatiable.

They broke apart finally, breathing hard, eyes on each other. Olivia was the first to break the standoff, reaching for the top button of his shirt. His breath caught in his throat as her knuckles brushed against his bare skin. He'd had a lot of women undress him, had had a lot of women period. But he had never held his breath as they'd done so. Had never anticipated a touch so much he'd almost jumped out of his skin by the time she'd freed all the buttons and slid her hands up his bare abdomen.

"You are the most beautiful man I have ever seen in my life," she murmured, tracing the ridges of his abs with her fingers. "And I've seen a few."

"I'd rather not hear about your ex-lovers," he growled. "I had one in my face tonight."

"On shoots," she reprimanded quietly. "Guillermo was my first and only lover."

That burned a searing path through him. If he hadn't hated the Venezuelan before, he did now. He didn't want to think about any man's hands on Olivia. Only his.

He dipped his shoulders as her fingers slid under the collar of his shirt and pushed it off. Thoughts about ex-lovers vanished as Olivia brought her mouth to his pecs and scored her lips and teeth across the width of him. When she had thoroughly tasted his skin, the ridges of his muscles that flexed beneath her touch, she brought her mouth to one of his nipples and teased it to erectness with soft, flicking motions of her tongue. He braced a hand against the window as she sucked it inside her mouth. *Cristo.* Helen of Troy had nothing on her.

She transferred her attention to his other nipple. He closed his eyes and let himself feel. Feel what this woman did to him, because he rarely, if ever, relinquished control in anything he did, but with her it was impossible not to.

"The photo Alessandra took of you," he rasped, a spasm of pleasure shaking him as she drew his nipple deeper inside her mouth. "That better have been me in your head."

She looked up at him, dragging her fingertips over his hard, burning nipples. "You made sure it was… Did you like it?"

"*Like* is an understatement."

He reached down, slid his arm beneath the curve of her hip and swung her up into his arms. She fit perfectly there, as if she was made for him. It intensified the skittery, antsy feeling he'd been experiencing all night. *Dangerous*, his senses told him. But tonight he wasn't listening to his head. Wasn't focusing on anything but slaking his lust until there was none left.

He carried her into the penthouse and into the bedroom, which had become a war zone between them, a symbol of their mutual antagonism. But not tonight. He set her down on the carpet and reached for his watch, his socks. Peeled them off with deliberate intent. Liv moved her hands to the straps of her dress.

"Nessuno." His quiet command brought her head up. He crooked a finger at her. "Come here."

She walked toward him, myriad emotions in her blue eyes. Anticipation, definitely. Uncertainty… *Maybe*. She stopped inches from where he stood, so close he could feel the warmth of her breath on his cheek. He ran the pad of his thumb across the generous sweep of her lower lip. "I haven't forgotten what you started in the restaurant that night, Liv. *Finish it*."

Her eyes widened. Hot color flamed her cheeks. He watched her mouth form words, but they never came. He wrapped his fingers around hers and brought them down to rest against the straining bulge beneath his trousers. "Sitting at that table that night, all I could picture was you touching me, *cara*." His fingers tightened over hers. "I burned for it. I burn for *you*."

Color infused her neck and chest now, touching every centimeter of her. A muscle worked convulsively in her throat as she brought her other hand down to join the one he'd placed there, her fingers working the leather strap free of his belt. She pulled hard, uncinching it. He sucked in a sharp breath. Then her fingers were undoing the top button of his trousers, pulling his zipper down. The remainder of his breath left his lungs as she slid her hands inside his pants to cup the length of him.

Maledizione. He closed his eyes. "That's it. *Just like that.*"

She moved her fingers up and down him, explored the hard length of his shaft molded by the close-fitting boxers he wore. Her touch goaded him onward, pushed him to an aching, desperate hardness. *"Di più,"* he murmured. *More.*

She slipped him out of his boxers and took him in her palms. He was big, harder than he'd ever been in his life, and her soft gasp made him swell even larger. "That's right, *cara*. You do that to me. Only you."

She ran her fingers up and down the pulsing length of him, taking her time to learn the contours of him, the silky tip of him. When he couldn't take it anymore, he allowed his eyes to slit open.

Her gaze locked with his. The lust he read there almost pushed him over the edge. "In your mouth, sweet Liv. Do it. *Now.*"

The last word came out ragged and hoarse. A plea as much as it was a command. She must have been as lost as he because she gathered him in her hands and did as he said. He tensed, his entire body going stiff. His first slide inside her hot, welcoming mouth almost unmanned him. He tipped his head back and focused on the cloudless, dark sky through the skylight as he pushed himself back from the edge, forced himself to last so he could enjoy the insane pleasure Olivia was lavishing on him with decadent sweeps of her tongue.

When she had taken him as far as he could allow without ending it right there and then, when his sanity was failing him, he buried his fingers in her hair and brought her to her feet. His own essence mixed with her sweetness as he kissed her was the most heady pleasure he'd ever experienced. But he knew it could be better. Much better.

Olivia returned Rocco's devouring kiss, her fingers buried in his hair, consumed with a sexual frustration, a need, the likes of which she'd never felt. He had built her up, played her, with such skill. Used her desire for him to inflame her own. And now she had to have him. *Desperately.*

Rocco lifted his mouth from hers, cupped her scalp in his fingers as his gaze meshed with hers. "You want me to touch you, beautiful Liv? Make you as crazy as you have made me?"

She could do nothing but nod mindlessly. He sat down on the bed and drew her between his legs. Her heart boomed in her chest, slamming against her ribs so hard she feared she might develop a heart condition right there and then. The strongest organ in her body felt as if it was going triple speed, the insistent pulse of it reaching into the base of her throat, making it hard to breathe. Her knees, which had just about had enough tonight, quivered at the carnal expression on Rocco's face as he took her in.

He reached up and slipped the straps of her dress off her shoulders. The lightest touch of his fingers on her skin made her shudder. A smile tipped his lips. "*Sì,* Liv. We either survive this or we go up in flames. But we do it together."

She was afraid it was going to be the latter. She was afraid she wasn't going to survive *him.* He tugged her to him, pushed the dress down over her hips and off. Her eyes followed the dress as it fell in a pool of silk at her feet instead of looking at him, because he was too intense for her to handle.

Rocco slid his fingers under her chin and brought her gaze back up to his. "You look at me. No hiding tonight."

He reached around, released the clasp of her bra and let it drop to the floor with her dress. His gaze moved down over her, lingering on the swell of her breasts, then her last remaining piece of clothing, a tiny navy blue lace thong. "Out," he growled, urging her out of the pool of her dress and bra and kicking them aside. Then he brought her back between his legs.

His gaze held hers as he slid his palm between her thighs. Her panties were damp, betraying her desire for him. She closed her eyes at the satisfaction that glittered in his eyes. His fingers tightened on her thighs. "Open them," he commanded. "Do not close your eyes to me, Olivia."

She did. She was pretty sure she would have done anything he asked right about now, she was that turned on. But it was excruciatingly hard to make herself look at him as his stare burned into hers. As he removed the sliver of damp material and ran his thumb along the wet seam of her most intimate part.

A low moan broke from her throat. *"Oh."*

He filled her with a finger then, his caress aided by just how intensely she wanted him. It was perfect, exactly what she needed when she was on fire for him.

"Like that, *cara*?"

"Yes." She gasped. "Just like that."

He brought his thumb to the center of her and rubbed her slowly, deliberately. She threw her head back and gave herself over to it. He left her alone for long moments while she pushed her hips against his hand and savored his delicious torment. But soon it wasn't enough. Not nearly enough.

"Rocco, *please*."

He stopped his delectable movements until her gaze was back on his. Then he eased another finger inside of her, filling her even more completely. She gasped as he invaded her tightness, stretched her body.

"I can feel you clenching around me, *mia cara*." His eyes were a hot, dark brown on hers. "Imagine how I will feel inside of you, filling you completely."

She already had when her hands had been all over him... She closed her eyes and focused on the rhythm he set, because now it really was too much. Concentrated on the release she craved. He slowed it down, drew out her pleasure until she almost screamed. Then he did it all over again. Faster, harder, he played her until heat infused every centimeter of her body and she was out of her head.

She didn't realize the animallike groan had come from her until he pulled his fingers from her, pushed her back on the bed and came down between her splayed thighs. She thought he might take her then, but he pushed her thighs farther apart instead, moved his broad shoulders between them and slid down her body until his warm breath fanned her thigh. *Oh, Lord.* His tongue skated over her hot, aching nub in the briefest of movements. She grabbed the bedspread with her hands and clenched it between her fingers.

His soft laughter filled the air. "Tell me, sweet Liv. I want to hear you say it."

She squeezed her eyes shut, too shy to say it. He slid two fingers inside of her again, penetrating her slow and easy. Driving her to distraction.

"Say it."

"Please."

"Please what?"

Her brain clouded over. "Your tongue," she groaned. "Your tongue... God, Rocco, please, I want it *there*."

He rewarded her with long, slow laps of his tongue that

built her pleasure to such an excruciatingly good level that it was almost, almost enough. But not quite. She begged him then, husky, broken entreaties that sounded so wanton to her ears she would have stopped if she hadn't been so desperate. But she was, and when he drove his fingers deeper and concentrated the expert flick of his tongue on the throbbing heart of her, she came apart beneath him like Fourth of July fireworks, pleasure radiating through every last centimeter of her skin.

She was incoherent, thanking him with broken sentences when he worked his way back up her body and took her mouth again with his. The intimacy of the kiss after what they had just shared was shattering.

"Sì," he growled thickly as they broke apart to breathe, his eyes blazing into hers. "It is the most perfect thing I have ever encountered. You and me, Olivia. How we taste together. How we fit together."

Her heart exploded in an emotion she had never felt. He was the most raw, sexual lover she could ever have imagined. But *this*, what they shared, was so much more than that. She closed her eyes to hide what she knew was blazing from them. To protect herself from *him*.

The sound of a foil wrapper being ripped open snapped her eyes wide. The way he slid the condom on the pulsing, thick length of him, his movements a sensuous caress, sent a hot wash of desire flaming back through her. She couldn't imagine coming again after what he'd just done to her, but looking at him on his knees like that made her insides quiver.

Rocco read her expression. *"Sì, bella,"* he murmured, hooking a heavy thigh over her and straddling her. "That was only a warm-up. You get more."

Her insides contracted, imagining him there, filling her. He took her mouth in a long, lingering kiss. Ran his palm down her leg to lift her thigh around his waist. "Take me inside you," he prompted in a throaty, raspy voice, his lips against hers. "Show me how much you want me, sweet Liv."

She reached down and wrapped her fingers around him, guiding him to her damp flesh. He eased inside of her with a gentle push, giving her time to accommodate his size and girth. She arched against him, demanding more. He pressed kisses against her mouth, told her how good she felt, giving her more and more of him until he was buried deep inside of her, and her body cried out at the fullness of it.

"*Cristo*. Liv." His gaze clung to hers as he held himself still. "You are so tight."

It was perfect. *He* was perfect. Her eyes told him so as he started to move. Her leg snaked tighter around his waist. The hypnotic quality of his lovemaking demanded her full and complete attention, and she gave it to him, savoring every deep drive of his body into hers.

"Tell me," he insisted, his gaze a hot brand on her face. "Tell me how I make you feel."

"So good," she moaned. "Like nothing I've ever felt before…"

Something passed between them then, deep and irretrievable. She saw it in his eyes, watched him register it before his face went blank; he lifted himself up on his forearms and took her with a fierceness that stole her breath. The show of pure strength sent her lust into overdrive. Her body pulsed back to life as his thick hardness caressed her insides. His eyes glittered as her face telegraphed her pleasure. "Touch yourself," he commanded. "I want to watch you make yourself come."

She squeezed her eyes shut, that particular demand a bit much for her even at this point. But his deep strokes were promising a release that wasn't coming, and she needed it badly. She moved her fingers between her thighs and against the hard nub of her. His low growl of approval reverberated in her ear. "That's it, *bella*. That is so sexy."

She stroked faster, harder, the deep throb of his body sending her close to a release she knew would break her. His breathing turned harsh in her ear, his strokes coming quicker, deeper, his rough encouragement in her ear spurring her on until she teetered on the edge.

"Now, Liv," he ordered hoarsely. "Come with me."

She sent herself over the edge with a desperate slide of her fingers against her throbbing flesh. His hoarse curse as his body swelled inside of her and he came amplified her mind-shatteringly good orgasm to make her whole body shake. He let his body cover hers, carried her through the storm until she stopped shaking and came out the other side.

They stayed like that, their bodies joined, for so long that her eyes drifted shut. The last thing she remembered before passing out from pure exhaustion was Rocco withdrawing from her, leaving the bed, then returning moments later to gather her in his arms and press her against his long, hard body. She felt safe then, safe to let go. So safe she ignored the fact that she had just given her soul away.

Rocco woke with his habitual insomnia at 2:00 a.m. This time, however, he lay with perfection in his arms. Olivia was curved into his side, fast asleep, his arm slung around her waist, her silky hair spilling across his chest.

He captured a lock of her hair in his fingers. Watched the moonlight play across its golden strands. The singularity of what they'd shared last night slammed into his head like the most potent of wake-up calls. His hand froze, tangled in the golden strands. What did he think he was doing? Did he actually even know?

Gingerly, silently, he slid out of bed and found his boxers lying on the floor. He slid them on, took a bottle of water out of the fridge and went out to the living room to settle in his favorite chair. It would be an hour or two before he found sleep again. It had been this way since he'd been a little boy. It had started after his mother had died and his father had gone out to gamble at night, leaving him and Alessandra alone in the house. Rocco had woken in the middle of the night to find his father still gone and paced the house, instinctively playing guard dog over Alessandra. Missing his mother terribly. He would stay up until he could no longer keep his eyes open or his father came home. Whichever happened first. Later when Giovanni had taken them to Villa Mondelli, he continued to wake at night. He would sit on the stone wall of the majestic house on the water and stare out at the silent, dark lake and mountains.

What a huge, dark world, he'd thought. Had his mother's essence been swallowed up by this massive, endless lake? Or was she still there looking over him? He'd ached for her those nights. Ached to have her warm, reassuring voice soothe him to sleep, not a nanny who wasn't the same. He'd dealt with his childish fear of the unknown by making up stories of friendly sea monsters who would come up to shore and take him to play in those dark depths, returning him before dawn.

Now in the middle of a New York night decades later, a full-grown man with the weight of the world on his shoulders, he craved the reprieve Olivia had given him last night.

In helping her to move through the darkness, to move on from the past, he had lost himself in her. He had allowed himself to take what he wanted, to hell with the consequences. And there would be consequences. His insides shifted, rearranging themselves in a foreign pattern he didn't recognize. He wasn't sure there was any going back from last night.

Wasn't sure he wanted to go back.

He tipped the water into his throat, welcoming the cool rush against his overheated senses. But of course he had to. Last night he had allowed himself Olivia because she'd needed him. Because they were in this together, as he'd promised her, and this wasn't just a deal to him anymore. But to allow himself to become more emotionally invested in a woman like Olivia, who needed someone to help her become whole again? Who needed to see her through the dark and the light? *Impossible.*

Even if she had the potential to be *the one*, he was incapable of love. "The one" didn't exist for him. Everyone he'd ever loved had left him in some form or another. His mother and Giovanni through death. His father through extreme neglect. Needing no one was the only way he knew how to cope. And Olivia? Olivia deserved more. *Someone like goddamn Guillermo Villanueva.*

Whose heart she had broken. He winced inwardly as he recalled the look on the other man's face when Olivia had walked into his arms. The guy was torn up. Olivia had that kind of an effect on a man.

He tilted his head back and took in the rough, unstructured skyline of Manhattan. He'd broken his promise to stay away from her. Perhaps that had always been inevitable, given the attraction between them. Given how emotional last night had been. He could tell himself he wouldn't touch her again, but he knew now he couldn't keep that promise. And maybe, he thought grimly, he'd been approaching this all wrong. Maybe he just needed to do like he did with all the other women in his life—allow himself as much as he wanted of Olivia with the knowledge that one morning he'd wake up and have had enough.

Olivia was alone in the bed when she woke, thirsty and disoriented. It came back to her in a rush. She was in New York, she had walked in Fashion Week last night and Rocco had pulled her out of the fire.

They had made love with an intensity she would never, ever be able to get out of her head.

The dark sky told her it was still the middle of the night. She put a hand out to touch the spot where Rocco had lain beside her and found it cool to the touch. He was up again. An insomniac who never seemed to sleep more than five hours a night.

She downed a glass of water, slipped on a T-shirt of Rocco's that was lying on a chair and went in search of him. He was in the living room, reclining in his favorite chair, staring up at the sky through the floor-to-ceiling windows.

"Why don't you sleep?"

He sat up, blinked hard as if he'd been in another world. "I've been this way since I was a boy. It's not a particular skill of mine."

He'd been minding the fort while his father had engaged in all sorts of debauchery. Protecting his sister. Giovanni had told her more than she'd ever admit to Rocco. How he had sheltered Alessandra from all the twists and turns in life and put himself last, always.

She moved closer, feeling braver with the connection they'd shared. Lines of fatigue depressed the skin around his eyes and mouth, his expression remote. His hair was rumpled, his only clothing the tight-fitting pair of boxers he'd worn earlier.

"You don't sleep because you're always on duty. With Mondelli. With your sister." With her. A pang filled her chest. "Alessandra is lucky to have you."

He lifted a shoulder, a naked, stunningly muscled shoulder that made her remember what he did with all that power. "She drew the short end of the stick when it came to a father. I couldn't make up for what Sandro did, but I did what I could."

"You did a lot. She adores you."

"We are…complicated."

Silence stretched between them. She didn't know

whether he wanted her to stay or go, so she remained rooted to the hardwood floor. A question came, unbidden. "Why didn't Giovanni leave you a controlling stake of Mondelli? It makes no sense."

He sat up straighter, his brows drawing together. "How do you know that?"

"I overheard it at Mondelli," she lied.

His expression darkened. "I have no idea what was going on in Giovanni's head when he made that decision."

"You think he didn't trust you."

His gaze narrowed on her, razor-sharp and infinitely dangerous now. "What makes you think that?"

Her teeth pulled at her lower lip. "It's a natural assumption. He didn't leave you a controlling stake. You wonder why. But that's not the case, Rocco. Giovanni thought you were utterly brilliant."

"More things you talked about?" His ebony eyes glittered in the moonlight. "He thought I was a loose cannon. That's why he did it."

She wrapped her arms around herself, a shiver making its way up her spine at the aggression emanating from him. "Everyone has limits. He felt sometimes you didn't recognize yours. No man is an island, Rocco. Although you try very hard to be."

The glitter in his eyes intensified. "Oh, but I am. Don't fool yourself, Olivia."

She recoiled from the sarcasm lacing his tone. It was a clear warning of where the line was. But fool that she was, she'd walked right over it last night, and it was a one-way street.

She might have left then, her skin stinging, but he snaked an arm out, captured her around the waist and dragged her down on his lap.

His gaze fused with hers. "While you're here…"

Held against all that delicious hard muscle, every centimeter of her skin burned with the impact of his on hers. Antagonism blended with want as she absorbed his erection pressing against her bottom. He was angry. She *should* walk away. But her body wasn't in agreement with her head. It was tightening, *remembering*, anticipating him.

Her breath jammed in her throat. Yanking it forcefully into her lungs she tried to resist. "Maybe we should…"

"Do it again." He slid his gray T-shirt up and cupped her breasts. The rasp of his thumbs over her nipples made every inch of her tighten. "I ignored these earlier," he murmured, his gaze hot on her skin. "A travesty. They are so…*fantastici*."

All thoughts of walking away fled as he rolled her nipples into hot, aching points between his fingers. She wanted him inside her again desperately. Craved the way he'd brought her such intense pleasure.

He lifted her up with the power of those amazing biceps and turned her so she was facing the skyline of Manhattan, her back against his hard, hot body.

"Rocco…" She didn't like that she couldn't see him. That he had complete control…

His hand slid between her thighs, his thumb making electric contact with her still-tender skin. She moistened where he touched, her body readying itself for his possession. "So responsive," he murmured in her ear. "You take me so perfectly, Olivia."

She closed her eyes and gripped the sides of the chair as he used her arousal to moisten her flesh, to slide over her in insistent, deliberate caresses that had her arching against his skillful fingers. He was hard, pulsing beneath her, promising heaven.

He sucked her earlobe into his mouth, the heated pull sending another shock to her core. "Tell me when you're ready for me," he murmured. "It will be deeper, more intense for you this way."

"What way?" Her words were a low croak, wrestled from her throat.

He removed his fingers from her, released himself from his boxers and sank his hands into her waist to lift her above him. She felt the hard pressure of his erection brushing against her.

"This way, *cara.*" He brought his mouth to her ear. "Take what you want."

She wanted all of him. She reached down and guided him into her. He lowered her slowly onto his hot, turgid flesh, his strong arms controlling the penetration. Which was a good thing—she gasped as he filled her—because he had been right. In this position he felt so big; she felt him *everywhere*. Unable to look at him, to experience this with him, all she could do was close her eyes and feel.

Rocco shifted his hands to her buttocks and took the weight of her in his palms. He was buried inside of her now, the sensation so wickedly good she dropped her head back on his shoulder and just breathed. His soft laughter filled her ear. "I told you you would like it."

He pushed her forward gently with a palm to the small of her back so she was angled forward. His hands took the weight of her buttocks again, lifting her up and down on him in a delicious rhythm that stole her breath. Every time she came back down on him, he filled her breathtakingly full, stroking every centimeter of her. And then her hips caught the rhythm. She increased the pace, taking him inside her, retreating, then claiming him again. His thumbs slid over the unbearably sensitive tips of her breasts, pinching and rolling.

She knew then that whatever this man asked of her, she would give him. It was that good between them.

His breath came harder in her ear, *strained*. She wanted to let go for both of them, but she couldn't get the friction she needed, not in this position. Frustration escaped her throat in a low mewl. Rocco brought her back against his chest, one arm wrapping around her waist to hold her secure. He slid his free hand between her legs and found her clitoris. She was crazy for him, arching against him uncontrollably as he rubbed two long fingers over her time and time again. "Come for me, *bella*."

One last press of his wicked fingers and she cried out, her release so intense and centered it was more like a scream. His mouth came down to smother the bulk of it in a long, hot kiss as he drew out the pleasure for her, made her rock against his fingers a second time.

His low groan filled her ear as she regained sanity. "I need a condom."

"I'm on the pill," she managed to get out. "It's fine."

His fingers bit into her hips, then, needing no second urging as he tipped her forward, filled her again and again with hard thrusts that made her release reverberate through her body. He chased his orgasm fast and hard, and it was explosive when it came, his essence filling her with a sweet, hot warmth that seemed to touch every part of her.

She wasn't sure how long it was—five, ten minutes perhaps—before he pulled his T-shirt over her head, cleaned them up and carried her back to bed.

Olivia wrapped herself around his big warm body and willed her complex, hardened lover to sleep. He passed out in her arms minutes later.

The triumphant, warm feeling that filled her at being able to soothe him was matched only by the stark, fairly terrifying knowledge that she was lost, totally irrevocably lost, to him. And he would likely never, ever return those feelings.

CHAPTER ELEVEN

ROCCO WAS CONSIDERING going in search of his fiancée with a Milan Fashion Week kickoff party on the agenda when Gabriella returned from an errand she'd been running for him and stuck her head in his office, a horrified look on her face.

"Did you forget your meeting with Renzo Rialto?"

His stomach plummeted. *Dio del cielo.* He had. He'd been fixing a last-minute seating glitch with the wedding planner.

"His PA just sent me a message to reschedule." Gabriella's gaze searched his face as if to say he'd been off lately and was he okay?

No, he wasn't, he decided, raking a hand through his already rumpled hair. In the week and a half since he and Olivia had been back from New York, his attempts to drown himself in his soon-to-be wife's charms and get her out of his system had failed miserably. If anything, he was falling harder.

He was distracted and antagonized, and it was a problem he couldn't seem to fix.

"I clear forgot," he said to Gabriella. "What did you tell Renzo's PA?"

"That you were detained in another meeting, were ever so sorry and would reschedule."

"Bene." He flashed her a smile, grateful for his PA's tact. But inside, his guts were churning. He and Renzo had

been meeting to discuss North American business strategy, a key priority for Mondelli in the coming year. His fingers tightened around the pen he was holding. Renzo would drag him over the coals for this. Ask him where his priorities were...

"Could you reschedule for next week, same time?"

Gabriella nodded and disappeared.

He threw down his pen, furious with himself. The damn wedding was turning into a beast he couldn't control. So was Olivia's stress. He'd watched her push her way through her fears to walk in London Fashion Week. Watched her brave press speculation she wasn't the model she had once been with rumors running rife about what had happened backstage in New York.

"She doesn't have her usual swagger," one commentator had pronounced. Panic Attacks Wreak Havoc on Top Model's Career blared another tabloid that had apparently been able to find someone backstage that night in New York who would talk.

Olivia had transgressed it all with a determined focus on the end goal that said she'd let it kill her before she gave up. She wanted her line. She wanted her dream. But the stress was clearly taking its toll. She was looking gaunt, she wasn't sleeping much and the tabloid viciousness was eating away at her like a slow-moving disease.

He stared vacantly at the original Monet on the wall opposite him, its magnificent colors and lighting a favorite of his. The light in *Olivia* was fading daily. And nothing he did seemed to help.

He ran his palms over his stinging eyes. It should make him happy his fiancée was keeping it together, because *his* future was just as intertwined with Olivia's success as hers was. The board was thrilled with the rise in Mondelli's stock price, business was booming with the brand's newfound cool factor and Olivia was the hottest name in the industry.

It seemed the more miserable Liv was, the more speculation surrounding her, the more the brand skyrocketed. His chest tightened with that interminable, inescapable guilt he had been feeling for weeks. It was like a two-edged sword he was constantly being impaled on.

The only time Olivia *was* happy was when she was in the studio with Mario creating. And in bed with him. And since that was also a source of confusion between them, because it could never be more than sex for him, and he could see from her eyes when they were together that it was more for her, he felt like the biggest bastard alive.

The late-afternoon sun spilled into the room, blinding him momentarily. He dropped his gaze to the pile of research he'd intended to take to his meeting with Renzo this afternoon, ironclad evidence Mondelli was on an upswing in the American market. He had never, ever forgotten a meeting in his career. Certainly nothing of this magnitude.

Where was his head?

A glittering jewel he couldn't resist... That was how Giovanni had described Tatum. And her daughter was that for him. His weakness.

It was what Renzo had been warning him about. About allowing his concentration to slip when he needed it most.

His mind took him back to that bottle of Scotch he and Giovanni had shared one summer evening at the villa as the sun set over the mountains. It had started out as a celebration of his new job as CEO, then devolved into a long, meandering discussion of life, one in which his grandfather had opened up like never before.

"Your father," he had stated baldly, "had much of you in him. Same razor-sharp brain, same instinct for business... But he has a weak streak a mile wide, and he allowed himself to be ruled by it."

Giovanni had turned his dark, wise gaze on Rocco, the younger man still shaking in his shoes at the responsibility he now carried. "He was my biggest shame, my biggest disappointment."

And that had been the last Giovanni had ever spoken of his son's failures. Rocco had gone on to be what his father hadn't, but always with the latent fear buried deep inside of him he might carry his father's flawed gene.

The antagonism that gripped him now was stark, clutched at his insides with insistent, grasping hands. Showing weakness like he did toward Olivia was a slippery slope down the path his father had traveled. Not only did she get to him like no other woman had, but her instability had the power to take him down with her.

He returned his gaze to the vibrant Monet. Somehow, some way, he had to stabilize the situation. Help Olivia help herself. And take back control with her while he was at it.

He picked up the tickets to the Fashion Week gala and headed for the studios. There would be more press there tonight. More opportunities for Olivia to go sideways. And frankly, he couldn't put her through it. Couldn't put himself through it watching her.

He found her in the studios with Mario and a group of young women seated around one of the large design tables. Ten sets of eyes planted on him in unison. *The mentoring program.* Olivia had mentioned to him on the drive in this morning it was starting today.

She caught his gaze and held up five fingers. He nodded and melted into the background, watching her from the sidelines. Her cheeks were flushed with an excitement he hadn't seen in weeks. Her joie de vivre, that brilliant smile of hers when she was in her element like this, made his breath constrict in his throat.

This was what she should be doing. Not walking a runway or posing for a camera, although she was amazing at that, too. She should be waking up with that smile on her face every morning instead of dreading the day.

He turned away and walked to the window facing the courtyard. That kind of thinking was ludicrous. He couldn't give Olivia what she needed on any level. Her name was turning Mondelli into a hot commodity, making the industry focus on her, and not the loss of Giovanni.

It was out of his control.

Olivia smiled and waved as the last of the women left the room, delaying the confrontation with her fiancé as long as she could. Brooding and unapproachable, he appeared to be in a filthy mood. *Wonderful*, since they had to spend the evening together making small talk.

Mario wandered off to talk to another designer. Rocco handed him something on the way out. Olivia studied his stormy gaze. "I can be dressed in five minutes. Where's your tux?"

"We aren't going."

"Really?" She tried to temper the excitement in her voice.

"Si."

"Why?"

"Because neither of us are up to it, and you need some sleep."

"I can do it," she protested. "I'm fine. Did something happen today?"

"Niente. I just think you need some rest. All anyone cares about is seeing you walk for Mondelli in Italy for the first time anyway, which will happen tomorrow. It's not necessary."

The familiar noose around her neck tightened. Never mind that her appearance in London had been flawless.

The press were out for blood... How long could she keep running before she cracked?

She swallowed her nerves back. "You aren't going to pepper me with wedding stuff, are you? The gala might be preferable." They were marrying in three and a half weeks after Paris Fashion Week, the last event of the season. Half the world was attending, and ever-in-control Rocco had it all under his thumb along with that efficient wedding planner of his.

Rocco gave her an even look. "Have you worked out your dress with Mario?"

"Yes." It was exquisite. The very dress she would have picked if she'd been marrying him for love. Which she was. But he didn't love her and it wasn't a real marriage, so more the fool for her for wasting her dream dress on a sham wedding.

"He's got Alessandra's dress under control, too." She'd asked Alessandra to be her maid of honor, as they'd gotten close these past few weeks, and somehow it just felt right with Petra gone.

His mouth twisted in a half smile. "Then you're free and clear. If you can put up with me for an evening."

Her whole body lit up like a Christmas tree at the thought of spending a real evening with him. Which was insane, really. She'd been latching on to that look she'd seen in his eyes that night in New York, the look she saw every now and again when they were making love. He cared. She wanted to turn it into love. She was a fool.

They ate fresh perch and baby potatoes, accompanied by a light pinot grigio, on the patio overlooking Lake Como. Olivia felt herself falling more in love with her fiancé with every minute that passed. When he was like this, when he was relaxed and not obsessed with business, he was that man she'd met in Navigli. Utterly, overwhelmingly gorgeous and charismatic.

Her stomach in knots, she gave up trying to eat and put her fork down.

"Finished?"

Rocco had pushed his plate away and was looking at her expectantly. She nodded. He stood up and held out his hand. "Bring your wine. I want to show you something."

They walked down the stone steps that descended from the twelfth-century villa into the waters of Lake Como. Flanked by two exquisite marble statues, they were formal steps, meant for receiving company by boat. Rocco sat down on them with his wine and tugged Olivia down beside him. The view as the sun set on the lake and sheer mountain face on the unseasonably warm evening was so utterly exquisite neither of them spoke for a long while.

"I used to come here at night," Rocco finally said. "When I couldn't sleep. We scattered my mother's ashes in this lake."

Her heart turned over in her chest.

"Everything seemed so big and vast at seven without two parents. I was trying to make sense of something that didn't *make sense* in my father's defection and my mother's death. To control the chaos around me. So I made up sea creatures, sea friends, to keep me company. My nanny found me asleep down here one morning. They were all panicked looking for me."

An ache in her throat joined the one in her chest. "You were doing your best to cope."

"*Sì.*"

She swallowed. "I bet they were pretty amazing sea creatures. What did they look like?"

His mouth twisted. "Big, green scary-looking things with scales and long tails. But they had great smiles. That used to make them okay."

She slid her hand into his free one, feeling its warmth

engulf her, soothe her as it always did. "You're telling me this because you want me to slay my dragons."

He turned his head, his dark gaze sinking into hers. "You've already slayed half of them, Olivia. Now slay the rest."

She thought about that long and hard, because she was doing her best. She had been for weeks. She wasn't as strong as him. He was a rock, and she was not.

"I'll try."

He stood up and insisted she go to bed.

Standing there, in her mere wisp of a nightie in their bedroom with its magnificent view of the glistening lake, she thought he might leave her then to go to work.

His gaze fused with hers in that electric connection they shared, the one he couldn't control even though he wanted to. He reached for her, tugging the wisp of silk over her head and bringing the heat of their bodies together.

He desired her, wanted her desperately; she could feel it in the intensity of his lovemaking as he deposited her on the bed and staked claim to every inch of her. But there was more. She saw that naked emotion on his face again now when he took her, their bodies fitting together perfectly.

Her heart stopped in her chest as she waited for him to say it. *Willed* him to say it. But then he turned his head away from her and buried his lips in her throat. Switched it off like he always did when she got too close.

Her heart stuttered back to life. Went back to where it should have been. If he hadn't said it now, that he loved her, he never would. It was time for her to start accepting that. Protecting herself against the inevitable. Because it was coming. The day he shut her out completely.

CHAPTER TWELVE

MILAN'S PIAZZA DUOMO, the city's central square, and home to the massive, silver-spired, Gothic Duomo Di Milano cathedral, was the site of Mondelli's opening night Fashion Week show. Lit with eclectic green-and-blue lighting that cast an otherworldly glow over the square, the buzz in the crowd was palpable as Rocco negotiated the crowds, heading for the tent that housed the models and his fiancée, who would open the show. The cobblestones reverberated beneath his feet, the air around him sizzling with an electric energy as Italy's revered fashion brand made its triumphant return to Fashion Week with its fall/winter Vivo collection.

Renzo Rialto waved him over, his wife by his side in the front row. Beautiful even in her sixties and perfectly coiffured, Veronique Rialto was the epitome of elegance with her short-cropped silver hair and black cocktail dress. Rocco bent and kissed her on each cheek, wondering what it was like to spend your life in a loveless marriage. He'd always thought if he did marry, it would be just that. But for some reason lately, he thought he'd be better off on his own when Olivia left.

Did Veronique know Rialto didn't love her? he wondered. That she had been used for her status... Did she care?

Veronique gave his arm a warm squeeze as she pulled back. "You are a magician, Rocco. Mondelli is all anyone can talk about these days. But then again—" she teased with a smile "—your lovely fiancée is doing all the work, it seems. I can't wait to see her wearing Mario tonight."

The guilt that had been eating away at him took another large bite of his insides. He needed to find Olivia and make sure she was okay. She'd been her usual mess this morning with the show looming.

He nodded to the couple. "Will you excuse me? I was just on my way to find her."

He wound his way around the rows of seats back to the tent that held the models and designers. It was filled with the usual preshow frenzied activity, bodies scurrying in all directions.

"Have you seen Olivia?" he asked one of the models.

"Bathroom," she said, stretching an elegant, slim arm toward the portable toilets. He strode toward them only to walk straight into his fiancée, who was so chalk white in the face his heart rate quadrupled. *"Va tutto bene?"* he asked her in Italian. *Are you all right?*

She nodded and started to walk past him. "I'm fine. The show's about to start."

"Olivia," he growled, catching her arm. "What's wrong?"

"I just puked my guts out," she rasped, shaking off his hand. "That's what's wrong."

The pounding music increased in volume. She started walking. "I need to go."

He watched her join the floor director at the front of the tent, her shoulders set back. Savanna stopped beside him. "I didn't know the reporter from *Fashion Report* had been given a backstage pass. She was all over Olivia before I got to them."

Great. He felt his internal temperature grow to dangerous proportions. "We need to watch these things more carefully."

Savanna nodded. "I know. I'm sorry, Rocco. The publicist should have warned me."

He took his seat for the show. Fury at that damn reporter who'd been hounding Olivia every waking minute burned through him. Fury at himself for not stopping it all. He might command a multibillion-dollar fashion empire, but he had never felt so helpless in his entire life.

A spotlight bathed the stage in Mondelli blue. Olivia posed motionless beneath it. Camera flashes popped from every direction, adding to her otherworldly appearance. Resplendent in a lime-green evening gown that left her entire back bare, her incredible hair cascading down her back in a curtain of gold, her eyes glittering like blue fire, she almost didn't seem real. Every curve of her beautiful body he coveted, every dip he ached to possess—but every night he had her, his desire for her only got worse. Because he could not have her truly—not when he was breaking her soul.

He could see it in her eyes as she got closer and trained her gaze on him. The fire in her was a message for him. She was done.

The end of the show came; the interviews happened. When the party started, he didn't even ask if they were attending, just bundled Olivia in the car and drove to the apartment.

Olivia headed straight for the heated gardens—her place of peace. He followed and found her sitting, staring into the rock pools. "What happened?"

She turned to face him. "*Fashion Report* is going to run a feature on me next week. They plan to interview several other models who have suffered from anxiety disorders to round the piece out, since I won't talk."

He brought his back teeth together. "I'll get an injunction. I won't let them run it."

A resigned expression twisted her face. "You were the

one who told me I can't keep running. Let it go, Rocco. It needs to happen. Then maybe they'll stop."

She was right; he knew it. He sat down beside her and rested his elbows on his knees.

"You of all people know the positive effect the dirt on me is having on Mondelli." Her tone was resolute. "People can't get enough. The only thing that can stop this for me is you releasing me from my contract. And since I know you won't do that, there's no point in having this discussion."

Frustration seared through him. "It's not a question of what I want—I *can't* do it, Olivia. You know that as well as I do. You were brilliant tonight. Why can't you just focus? Do exactly what you did tonight and, after Paris next week, this will all be over."

Her mouth twisted. "And then there's the spring/summer shows. It will never stop until I'm out."

"You agreed to do this," he pointed out harshly. "You know you have to wrestle these demons of yours. Me pulling you from this campaign, making *me* the bad guy, won't help you do that. It will only make you feel like a failure. And that will hurt you more than those reporters ever could."

Her eyes flashed that blue fire they'd spit at him onstage. "*I* am not *you*. I am not some impenetrable force that can cut off my emotions at will, who puts work above everything else."

He rocked back on his heels, her accusations hitting him like a blow to the chest. "I do *not* put business above everything else. I have been by your side every minute these past few weeks when you needed me, Olivia. I have been there for my family *my entire life*. So do not say I don't care."

Her gaze drilled into him. "You are making me your wife for the sake of your company, Rocco. How much more evidence do you need that you are married to Mondelli?"

"I do not feel," he bit out, "that sacrificing a year of my

life is too much to do for the company I've built into an international powerhouse. A symbol beloved and revered by all Italians."

She nodded. "Exactly my point. It isn't a problem because you will never allow yourself to feel. You won't even talk to your father because you're afraid he'll be the kryptonite that fells you."

His gaze narrowed. "Are we talking about something other than our deal? Because the way I remember it, you were right there with me. You agreed to marry me because you don't believe in the concept of love."

Her shoulders slumped. "That was before I met you, Rocco. Before I let myself get to know the part of you that you don't bury ten miles deep."

His chest seized. "Olivia…"

"No." She cut him off with a wave of her hand. "You don't get to hide on this one. You know I'm in love with you. I've been in love with you since that night in New York when you pulled your pumpkin carriage up to the Lincoln Center and saved my soul like the fairy-tale hero you are. Actually—" she pursed her mouth "—maybe it was before that, maybe it was that night in Navigli when you rocked up to my table, sat down and blew my mind apart with your intellect and charm." She held his gaze, regret in her blue eyes. "But none of that really matters, does it? I've gone and done the unforgivable. I've fallen in love with a Mondelli, and that only ever ends in heartbreak for the Fitzgerald women."

He took a step toward her. She moved back with a shake of her head. "You don't get to solve this one with sex, Rocco. You don't get to sweep me off my feet and use that superior skill of yours on me, because we both know you can do it. We both know you *will* do it if I let you." She held her hands up. "This is me saying I'm done. Walking away from my addiction."

"*Maledizione*. Olivia." His hands dropped to his sides. "What do you want me to say? Do you want me to say I care about you, because you know I do?"

Her eyes dimmed. "If you cared about me, you would set me free. You would allow yourself to tell me how you really feel. Because only a fool would spend the rest of her life pining away for a man who's always going to put her second to his real marriage."

He worked his jaw. "You are asking for the impossible."

A sad smile curved her lips. "Funny, Giovanni always told me to reach for the impossible. I'm surprised he didn't teach you the same."

She stood up. "I will do Paris next week and then I'm reevaluating. *Everything*."

The hair on the back of his neck rose, his stomach hardening to stone. "We are marrying in front of five hundred people in three weeks, Olivia."

She lifted her chin. "That was included in the everything."

"Olivia." He growled the warning at her.

She nodded. "I know. You will make me rue the day I put pen to paper." Her bleak gaze held his. "The thing is, I'm terrified if I follow through with this. If I make myself last this year, there will be nothing left of me at the end. And then what does it really matter?"

She turned and walked away. He let her go. Because she *was* asking for the impossible, and he couldn't give it to her no matter how much he wanted to. He'd been over it in his head a million times, and he'd still come up with the same answer. Taking Olivia out of the ten-million-dollar Vivo campaign would be brand suicide. It would destabilize Mondelli when it was still rocking from the loss of Giovanni.

His fingers bit into his thighs, his knuckles gleaming white. His feelings didn't matter in this. Duty over his freedom. It was the way it had always been. He could only hope that his fiancée carried out hers. Because this wedding was a machine that couldn't be stopped. It was a multimillion-dollar affair with implications way beyond the two of them. It would determine his future. The future of Mondelli.

CHAPTER THIRTEEN

OLIVIA SPENT THE days leading up to Paris Fashion Week at the apartment in Milan, avoiding her fiancé, who reluctantly agreed to give her space. She kept herself busy working with Mario on her designs while mentally preparing herself for one last walk down a runway. After that she truly didn't know what she was going to do. There was also that walk down an aisle with a man who didn't love her looming—and her head to get in order.

The *Fashion Report* segment aired the night before Paris. She watched the in-depth exposé on the pressures models faced in a world that valued perfection above all else in her hotel room alone, having insisted Rocco stay home. In some ways, the airing of her most private fears, the knowledge that she wasn't alone, helped a great deal. On another level, the fact that the whole world was now intimate with her private terror made Paris fifty times more intimidating.

She made it through the show with sheer willpower and the knowledge that if she chose to end things now she'd never have to walk a runway again. And yes, because she loved her fiancée and she didn't want to let him down. Then she did as she'd promised and took the time she needed. Instead of following Rocco's summons to board the Mondelli jet at Charles de Gaulle the morning after the show, she caught a flight bound for New York.

It was the last place she wanted to be. But if slaying her demons was her goal, it had to be done.

Her mother, busy packing for her wedding and a two-week vacation, took one look at her and opened a bottle of wine. "Please tell me you're not having second thoughts," she murmured, settling herself in the sofa across from Olivia in the Chelsea apartment she'd bought with her daughter's money.

Olivia took a sip of her wine. "Why? Because you can't bear for the gravy train to end?"

Her mother, whose poise was usually ironclad, flushed a deep red. "I deserve that, I know it. I let things get out of hand." She gave her an imploring look. "I didn't know. I swear I didn't know how dire things were or I never would have…"

"It doesn't matter." Olivia cut her off with a wave of her hand. And it really didn't anymore. "I forgive you for the money. What I can't forgive you for is never being there for me. For pushing me when you knew I was on the edge."

Her mother's gaze fell away from hers, making an elaborate study of the ruby-red liquid in her glass. "It was wrong. But I thought you were like me, Livvie. I thought you thrived on the excitement."

"I was having panic attacks at fifteen." Olivia threw the words at her in disbelief. "How did that make you think I was coping well?"

Her mother was silent at her outburst. Then she nodded. "You're right. I've been self-involved my entire life. It was the only way I knew how to be."

"Including Giovanni," Olivia challenged.

Her mother's surgically enhanced mouth tightened. "Including Giovanni."

Olivia tucked her legs underneath her and took a sip of her wine. "Tell me about what happened with him."

Her mother shrugged a slim shoulder. "I was in love with him."

"Mother." Olivia pressed her hands to her temples and massaged her throbbing head. "I did not fly thousands of miles for you to feed me the same lines you always do. You tore my life apart over him. I don't have a father because of him. Give me *something*."

Her mother's lips pressed into a straight line. "He was everything I ever wanted and everything I couldn't have. I knew it, I told myself not to do it, and when he left I wanted to curl up in a ball and die."

It was the most emotion she'd witnessed in her mother in a decade, and it knocked her back against the sofa for a moment. "What about his wife? Did you ever think of her? How she must have felt?"

Her mother's long lashes settled down over her blue eyes, identical to hers. "It wasn't that kind of love, Olivia. It was the once-in-a-lifetime kind. Giovanni and I were both starstruck. There wasn't any rationality to it."

Like her and Rocco.

She chewed on her lip. "I still don't understand what you were thinking. He was a married man." *Unobtainable.* "Why put yourself through that?"

Her mother shook her head. "I thought he'd choose me. I was *convinced* he would choose me. There was no other alternative."

And yet he hadn't. Giovanni had walked out of her mother's life without a backward glance and crushed her. Her mother had married her father and broken his heart, unrequited love at its most bittersweet.

It was why she'd walked away from Rocco. The fear that what she saw in his eyes might never translate into what she felt.

She stared at her mother. At the fragility she'd never seen in her eyes. And finally she understood why she was the way she was. To lose that kind of love did that to a person.

"If you could go back," she asked, "would you do it differently?"

Her mother shook her head. "This isn't me we're talking about, Olivia. Giovanni and I made our decisions. It's you and your inability to let yourself be vulnerable that is at issue here. And yes, I realize much of the blame for that stems from me. I wasn't there for you and I abused your trust. But," she said, "I can tell you one thing. I saw how you looked at Guillermo when you were with him and I see how you look at Rocco, and there is no comparison. You *love* him. And he is marrying you. So what's the problem?"

It wasn't a real marriage; that was the problem. But even as she said it she knew that wasn't true on so many levels. Everything on the surface between her and Rocco had ostensibly been about their deal, but none of it ever had, really. The raw emotion and passion between them was *real*. The naked emotion on his face when she'd boarded that jet for Paris had been real. The walls that had come down in New York that night had been real.

It is the most perfect thing I have ever encountered. You and me, Olivia. How we taste together. How we fit together.

Her stomach contracted in a long, insistent pull. He loved her. She knew he did. He just didn't know how to say it. He was too busy slaying her dragons, slaying everyone else's dragons, to figure it out.

Maybe he just needed an adult version of his yellow-eyed sea creature to come and rescue him. Maybe the unanswered calls on her cell phone from him weren't about him tracking down an asset, but him needing her as much as she needed him.

Hot liquid burned the backs of her eyes, blurring her

vision. She needed to talk to him. To see him. But there was one more thing she needed to do first.

She looked at her mother. "Will you take a drive with me?"

Her mother blinked. "You're getting married in two days, Olivia."

"I know."

Rocco stood on the runway in the blazing Milanese sunshine, a bouquet of calla lilies in his hand. He knew they were Olivia's favorite from what little input she'd given on her wedding bouquet. What he didn't know exactly was what he was doing here with them in his hands.

His eyes picked up the blue-and-white Mondelli jet banking its way through the clouds, his heartbeat increasing in anticipation along with it. Why he'd ever let Olivia go to Paris alone he didn't know. He'd watched that *Fashion Report* piece sitting in the den at the villa while Olivia prepared to walk in Paris and he'd physically hated himself in that moment. He had glossed over her anxiety, told her to be tougher when he could have shut her down completely in his zealousness to see Mondelli fly.

What did that say about him? That Olivia was right? That he put business above everything else in his life? That he was a machine programmed to do only one thing?

He rubbed a hand over his face as the jet turned and made its final approach, a fatigue it seemed he'd had his whole life making his limbs feel heavy and sluggish. The past few weeks had been hell. He had buried himself in work, told himself it was better this way with distance between him and Olivia, when all he'd really wanted to do was bury himself in *her*. And not just in a sexual way. She brightened everything about his life every minute she was in it, and he'd been numb without her. Witness the morning he'd just spent in board meetings going over insanely good

financials that should have left him pumped and victori-
ous, but instead had made his eyes glaze over. What did
any of it matter if he didn't have anyone to share it with?
And not just any woman, but the woman who had come
to mean everything to him.

He *had* made work his entire life. It had been necessary
to ensure his family business thrived. He'd sacrificed his
own happiness willingly because, he could admit now, he
had been too frightened to admit he had needs. That he
had the ability to love like everyone else. Because doing
so would have made him have to face his choices. Would
have made him vulnerable. And it was the one emotion
he could not tolerate.

The jet's nose pointed down as it swooped toward the
asphalt. His stomach went right along with it. He'd told
himself giving Olivia space would allow her perspective.
Perspective about what? About the words he couldn't say?
About the lies he'd been telling himself again and again?

His shame sank deeper. He had branded Olivia a cow-
ard when *she* had been the one courageous enough to tell
him how she felt. Because he did love her. The only reason he'd agreed to this marriage was because, deep down,
he did want to marry her. He wanted to have her. Protect
her. Be that heroic figure she needed.

The jet touched down on the tarmac and taxied to the
terminal. He waited at the bottom of the steps while the
crew secured the plane and opened the doors. The two
Mondelli designers who'd accompanied Olivia to Paris disembarked. He greeted them, then rested his elbow on the
railing of the steps as he waited for Olivia to emerge. The
designers gave him a funny look as they walked toward the
terminal. Chris, his pilot, appeared in the doorway, gave
the flowers in his hand a glance and came down a couple
of steps. "I, um…" He raked a hand through his hair. "Did
Olivia not tell you she was taking another flight?"

"Mi scusi?"

The pilot's face reddened. "She's not with us, Rocco. She said she was taking a break before heading home. I thought you knew."

His heart went into free fall. He'd thought she'd already had a break. That she was coming home to talk this over...

He had given her too much time. He had given himself too much time.

He narrowed his gaze on his pilot. "Tell me exactly what she said."

Chris handed him an envelope. "She asked me to give this to you."

His heart pounded as he tore open the envelope. It took no time to read the short message in Olivia's handwriting because it was only three sentences.

I have some things I need to do in New York. I need time to think, Rocco. Give it to me.

Disbelief blanketed him. They were marrying in front of five hundred people in two days, and she was in *New York*?

Was she even coming back?

He left, shoving the bouquet of lilies at a bewildered terminal attendant as he exited the building. He hadn't known much about what he was going to say to Olivia, but he had known he was going to be honest about his feelings. And he was going to release her from her contract. Set her free.

Poor, unsuspecting Adamo was the first person to see him upon his return to the Mondelli offices. *"What?"* Rocco bit out, dropping his briefcase on the floor.

Adamo set an envelope on his desk. "The prenuptial agreement is finalized."

Perfetto. The bitter irony of it hit him like a block to the head. The bride was missing and a document that was now not worth the paper it was printed on was ready. He picked it up and tossed it in the shredding bin. If he was marrying Olivia, there would be none of that between them, only her and him.

Adamo gave him a long look. "I also have something else for you."

Rocco's gaze swung to him. "I would suggest later is a better time."

Adamo laid a smaller envelope on his desk. It had an ornate *G* inscribed on the upper right-hand corner. *Giovanni's personal stationery.* Rocco stared at it. Now he was haunting him from the dead…

He lifted his gaze to the lawyer. "Where did that come from?"

"Giovanni told me to give it to you before your wedding day."

Maybe he should give it back given that wasn't likely to happen.

He gave Adamo a curt thanks and waved him out of his office. The envelope beckoned from the desk. It was sealed. He wasn't actually sure he could take its contents right now, but his curiosity overcame him and he sliced it open.

My dearest grandson Rocco,
When you receive this letter I will have passed from this world to the other side. You of all people will know that this is actually a blessing for me, because I get to be with my Rosa again. There has been an ache in my heart ever since she left me, and now I will be whole again.

By this time you will also have discovered the story of Tatum and myself through Olivia. It was never my intention to disrespect the love of my life. I know you will find this a particularly difficult pill to swallow, Rocco, as honor is the code you live your life by. However, I hope you will get to experience what it feels like to love like this someday and come to understand my actions. I never thought I could love two people with the depth that I have. None of my actions were taken easily, and I hope in resolving this as I did, any heartbreak I caused was minimized.

I know you will be questioning why I did not leave you control of Mondelli, and it was not, as I suspect you will think, because I do not trust you. You have more strength than your father and me combined— you always have. I wanted to give you the time to explore yourself. To learn that to love is not a weakness, but a strength. You have it in your heart, *nipote*, I have no doubt. We Mondellis love big and wholeheartedly. And you will, too.

Be kind to Olivia, who needs to be loved unconditionally after what she has been through. I know you have this in you, too, which is why I entrusted her to you.

Finally, walk lightly, Rocco, and remember the power of your actions. You carry a heavier stick than even you know.

Giovanni xx

Something frayed and weakened inside of Rocco tore open. He sat there for a long moment, heat burning the backs of his eyes. The questions he'd been asking for weeks had found answers, the niggling uncertainties that had made it even more difficult to sleep at night eased. He couldn't say he approved of all of his grandfather's decisions; Giovanni had been right on that. But his thoughts on where he was at the moment, his feelings for Olivia, rang uncannily true.

The fact that he had found his capacity to feel with Olivia was a potential his grandfather had foreseen. The fact that he had messed it up so badly was his to own and his alone.

He sat staring at the letter. Every bone in his body told him to go find Olivia and fix them. He had been fixing things his entire life. But she had said she needed time, and he risked losing her forever if he went after her. So all he could hope was that she showed up for this bloody circus of a wedding of theirs so he could say the words he needed to say.

If he'd thought he'd felt helpless before, that had nothing on this.

CHAPTER FOURTEEN

THE WEDDING DAY of Rocco Mondelli and Olivia Fitzgerald dawned crisp and clear on the shores of Lake Como in the shadow of the Alps. Referred to by the ancient poet Virgil as "our greatest lake," Lake Como was Europe's deepest at over thirteen hundred feet in depth, its deep blue waters stretching for a majestic thirty miles in length.

A perfect setting for the wedding that was capturing headlines around the world, Rocco thought, standing on the front steps of Villa Mondelli, the historic former Cistercian nunnery dedicated to the Holy Virgin. Except with four hours to go before the nuptials began, the palatial villa and grounds a hive of frenzied activity, one key component was missing. His bride.

He took in the two priceless carved statues of the Holy Virgin flanking the pillars of the front stairs and wondered if *she* was the problem. Maybe the wedding was on the rocks because no Mondelli had ever dared get married here given the villa's sacrosanct past. Maybe the nuns were protesting...

He rubbed a hand over his jaw and swept aside the dark humor. Because really nothing was humorous about being stood up at the altar. About suffering the ultimate public humiliation in front of five hundred guests from every corner of the world.

Stefan Bianco, Christian Markos and Zayed Al Afzal, resplendent in designer tuxedos and mauve bow ties to match the maid of honor's dress, stood beside him, all with identical expressions on their faces. Christian would call it the "what the hell do we do now?" look. Stefan, however, would have added a slightly more vicious edge to it, he knew. "I said she was trouble," he'd muttered last night when they'd arrived at the villa to find Olivia Fitzgerald was nowhere to be found twenty-four hours before the wedding. Zayed, the future king, had looked shocked. Which had now faded into his "ready for anything" expression, fitting for a man whose nation might soon be at war.

Three warriors who had conquered global markets and more than their fair share of hearts—and there was nothing they could do to make this right.

Christian frowned. "What next?"

Rocco shrugged, far more casually than the turmoil racking him inside. "If she loves me, she'll come."

"A good point," Zayed agreed.

"Goddamn her," Stefan exploded, turning on the future king. "This is not okay, *fratelli*. I want to find her and strangle her with my bare hands."

"That would not help the situation," Zayed countered. "Clear thinking is what is called for."

"And what," Stefan bit out, "would your *clear-thinking* head suggest? Five hundred people are on their way here *right now. The Pope*, a personal friend of the Mondelli family, is coming. And we are minus a bride."

"I'm going to drive into Milan and check the apartment." Rocco voiced the only solution he had left. "She loves the gardens there. It's a possibility."

"It's also a possibility she might use her phone," Stefan exploded, throwing his hands in the air.

Rocco gave him a look. He knew Olivia was on Italian soil. Her flight had landed early this morning in Milan. What she was doing now was another question. He intended to find out.

"Stay here with Zayed and keep things running," he instructed his hotheaded friend. "Make sure what needs to happen happens. You," he said, tossing his car keys at Christian, "drive."

He didn't trust himself to. Not now. When he'd decided to give Olivia her time to think, he hadn't meant *this*. He had things to say to her, important things to say to her, before they walked down that aisle. *If* they walked down that aisle. And he needed to be articulate about it.

He and Christian walked through the preceremony madness to the far driveway. The lead singer of Olivia's favorite rock group ambled across the lawn, a cigarette hanging out of his mouth. Chairs were arranged in endless rows of white against the sweep of green facing the lake. The ceremony would take place on its shore.

He steadfastly ignored it all, sliding into the passenger seat of the Aventador beside Christian. Just over an hour later they walked into the Milanese apartment. The housekeeper gave him a scandalized look and asked what he was doing there, then relayed the information that no, Olivia was not there. She hadn't seen her in a week.

Rocco mopped his brow. They were on their way out when his cell phone rang. He fished it out of his pocket, heart pounding, only to see it was Stefan.

"I thought you might like to know your fiancée is in the building. Well, actually," he drawled, "not anymore. Alessandra and the wedding planner have whisked her off to wherever she's supposed to be. That is, if you still want to marry her, because I can pass on a message. I would be *thrilled* to."

Rocco's pounding heart stopped in his chest. When it started again, he pressed the phone tighter to his ear. "Do not say *one word* to her. We're on our way."

As if anything else could go wrong, the main highway to Como was blocked by an accident on their return. They took the alternate, smaller highway, and this time Rocco commanded the wheel of the Aventador, pushed the pedal to the floor and prayed for time.

"They're on their way back."

Olivia peeled her gaze from the clear blue waters of Lake Como and nodded at Alessandra. After she'd spent the night with her mother in New York, they had driven to Brooklyn to banish Olivia's final demon. She hadn't been able to make herself visit Petra's grave because to do so would be admitting she was gone. But she'd realized now, it was preventing her from moving on. And if she was to face this day with what was truly in her heart, she'd had to let her go.

It had been painful and tougher than she'd expected. But she'd left New York with the feeling the city would no longer haunt her. That she could come back to visit. And maybe it had been the first step in repairing her relationship with her mother.

They had arrived in Italy early this morning. Even though her heart had known what it had wanted, her head had been engaged in a final desperate effort to protect itself. Rocco might hurt her. But was that worth a lifetime of wondering if she'd let the love of her life slip away?

She'd finally made up her mind and arrived here hours ago, only to find Rocco and Christian engaged in a wild-goose chase to find her. Guilt had set in. Then panic as Alessandra and the wedding planner had rushed her off to the neighbor's villa to get dressed prior to her arrival at the ceremony by boat. She hadn't intended to leave it this late. She needed to talk to Rocco. *And no one was listening to her.*

"Please," she said one more time to the wedding planner ninety minutes later as the flustered-looking blonde announced the men were back. "I need five minutes with Rocco."

"Not doable," the planner replied. "There are dignitaries who have to leave as soon as the ceremony is over, the fireworks are scheduled and we're already almost half an hour late." Her mouth compressed. "I told this to the men's camp, too. You have the rest of your lives to talk once this is done, so please, *focus*."

Rocco wanted to talk to her, too? Olivia started to argue, but the planner cut her off with a tersely delivered request to get her shoes on. She slid them on, pulled in a breath as Alessandra slipped her veil into place and straightened her shoulders. She *was* going to marry Rocco. She'd spent her entire life thinking she couldn't rely on anyone but herself, refusing to allow herself to love. But now she was going to take a leap of faith, because she knew with Rocco by her side she could do anything.

If he didn't kill her first for doing this.

The spray of the water split to the left and the right of the covered speedboat they rode in as Olivia and Alessandra were spirited toward Villa Mondelli. The sight of hundreds of wedding guests seated in chairs on the lawn, many of them foreign dignitaries she had never met, had her heart slamming against her chest as they neared the ornate front steps of the villa where Rocco's sea creatures had visited.

Her first priority as they docked was ensuring she had enough oxygen in her lungs to get through this without passing out. Second was getting out of the boat without tripping and falling flat on her face in the exquisite dress with the long flowing train Mario had made her.

Third was the man standing a hundred feet in front of her as she stepped out of the boat with the help of the waiting attendant. Flanked by the priest, Christian Markos,

Zayed Al Afzal and Stefan Bianco, Rocco was so ridiculously handsome in his tux it stole what little breath she had left. Her gaze locked on his but he was too far away for her to read the emotion in his eyes. Her knees wavered. *What if he didn't love her?*

The quartet started playing Pachelbel's "Canon." The tears she'd been holding back threatened. She blinked them away furiously, her hands clutching her bouquet of lilies. Alessandra started down the aisle, stunning in Mario's silk lavender creation, followed by their three flower girls in matching lavender dresses. Olivia's heartbeat accelerated in tandem with the further weakening of her knees. Her decision to give herself away seemed ill-advised now as her legs shook. She wished desperately she had something to hang on to. The aisle seemed a mile long and she *couldn't read his eyes*.

The cue for her to move came and went. And suddenly she knew she had to know what he was feeling, *see him*, before she took another step.

The panic that plummeted through Rocco at the sight of Olivia frozen at the end of the red-carpeted aisle was of the all-consuming fashion.

A sheen of perspiration broke out on his brow. His feet felt heavy, weighted down, as he willed her to start moving. His heart didn't seem to know how to beat. It hung in suspended animation for a long moment, then thudded heavily against his chest. *Nothing.* He kept his gaze on her as the music played on, ignoring the murmurs that swept the crowd. She looked so beautiful in the sleek gown Mario had designed for her. It was the one detail he hadn't planned. The one surprise from today, other than the fact that she almost hadn't shown up.

Done in off white, the sheer gossamer fabric clung to every curve, setting off Olivia's honeyed skin to perfection. It fell to the ground in a tulip-shaped hem, her long beautiful hair left loose, floating around her shoulders.

She looked like a mermaid come to life. His mermaid emerging from the steps he'd sat on as a boy, a living, breathing piece of perfection who had come to save the man.

Stefan's low curse pierced his haze. *She wasn't moving.*

"Now might be a good time to do something," Christian murmured. But Rocco was already moving, striding down the aisle toward Olivia. The murmurs came to a crashing halt, all eyes on him.

He kept his gaze on Olivia as he stopped in front of her and took her hands in his. They were ice-cold despite the warmth of the day. Her gaze fastened onto his, blue eyes wide and brilliant.

"You came," he murmured.

"I did," she said softly, her fingers tightening around his until she had a death grip on him. "I'm sorry to be so late. You look so very handsome."

"And you," he returned huskily, emotion overcoming him, "look like my very own mermaid come to life. Tell me you're staying."

She looked down at her dress with a tentative smile. "I don't have any scales, and green wasn't appropriate, but I do love you, Rocco. I'd like to help you slay your dragons if you'll let me."

He felt the world sway beneath his feet as everything became right with those few simple words from her. He absorbed them for a moment, savored them for the precious things they were, then blinked to clear his head and brought her hand to his mouth. "I didn't think I was going to get a chance to tell you how I feel," he murmured against her knuckles.

Her eyes remained glued to his. "Tell me. I need to hear it."

He lowered their hands and brought his mouth to her

ear. "Olivia Fitzgerald, I have been desperately in love with you since the night you walked off that stage in New York and into my arms. And if you'd walked into Guillermo Villanueva's, I would have taken him apart. No one is supposed to have you but me."

She melted into him. He kept talking, because he needed to get it out. "You were right. I have always put work first because I was afraid of turning into my father. Of being weak. Of getting hurt. But then you came into my life and I had no choice. You got to me in every way."

"Rocco…"

He leaned back and put a finger to her mouth. "I'm releasing you from the contract. Whether you decide to marry me or not. Focus on your work with Mario, bring your and Giovanni's line to market and make me proud. That's all I care about. All I care about is you."

Her eyes glistened. "The thing is, I've been thinking that I want to do it. For you. I went to see her grave, Rocco, Petra's, and I've let her go now. I think I needed to do that before I could move on."

He shook his head. "All I've done is push you. I won't lose you, Olivia."

A tremulous smile curved her lips. "You won't lose me. *I'm* the only person who can lose me. And it won't happen if I have you."

He rested his forehead against hers as the music drew to a close. "Do you think we could argue about this later? That is, if you are going to marry me today, because I think we should do that now."

That brilliant smile he loved lit her face, and in that moment he knew everything he'd ever wanted was within his grasp. She nodded and kept her forehead pressed to his. "Just you and me walking down an aisle, right? Nothing to it."

He smiled against her lips. "Nothing to it."

His heart ached with an almost unbearable pressure as he changed his grip on Olivia's hand so she was standing by his side. He nodded at the wedding planner, who looked as if she was on the verge of passing out. The music intended for their walk the other way played, and it didn't matter. Nothing mattered as the rather stunned-looking priest began the ceremony. Rocco held Olivia's hand throughout it, afraid to let her go.

He restrained himself, just, as they exchanged rings and the priest pronounced them husband and wife. The opportunity to kiss her had been too long coming, and he made the most of it. Christian made a joke about them getting a room. Rocco let Olivia go reluctantly. Later he would have her, and this time it would be with nothing but the truth between them.

Applause broke out as they walked back down the aisle as husband and wife. Perhaps unusual for such an elegant affair, but on a day like this, anything could happen.

Olivia didn't recall much of what occurred after Rocco told her he loved her. There was the receiving line full of his relatives, her parents, friends, dignitaries, celebrities and the *Pope*. There were canapés and champagne while they took photographs and a six-course dinner served in the ballroom as the night chill set in.

She and Rocco sat at a table with Stefan, Zayed, Christian, Alessandra, Violetta and Sophia. Olivia was grateful for her girlfriends' presence when Stefan was seated beside her. He had been glowering at her since the reception started, and had murmured in her ear she was damn lucky she made his friend so happy. She was more than relieved to turn Mr. Glower over to stunning-looking Violetta and Sophia in beautiful gowns, who charmed the pants off him and Zayed. Christian and Alessandra remained much more low-key, a surprisingly quiet corner of the table.

Her mother, assigned to keep Sandro Mondelli in line at the table next to them, was doing a fabulous job in her duties while multitasking by flirting with a widowed Saudi prince. Her father and his wife, on the other hand, looked a bit awkward sitting at their table with some of Rocco's relatives, but as the night went on seemed to loosen up and enjoy themselves.

When Rocco drew her to her feet for their first dance, Olivia's eyes nearly popped out of her head as Darius Montagne, the aging rock star she had been infatuated with since she was a teenager, took the stage solo with a guitar.

"Oh, my God. You did not."

"I did." He captured her hand and led her to the middle of the dance floor, where the spotlight picked them up. "And if you give him one sideways look I'll send him packing."

She moved into his arms, finding that funny given how mad she was about the man she had just married. "Oh, Rocco," she murmured, lacing her fingers through his and swaying into his embrace. "I think you underestimate how badly I have it for you."

He pulled her closer to his powerful body as Darius Montagne began singing a ballad. "Forgive me for acting a bit possessive," he growled, "because up until a couple of hours ago, I wasn't sure on that point."

"I told you I loved you on the balcony that night."

"That was a lifetime ago."

"I'm sorry." She burrowed closer to him. "One could look at it as suitable payback for that night in Navigli if one were so inclined."

"One could," he returned softly, his mouth at her ear. "One could expect retribution for that, too. Very *pleasurable* retribution."

A shiver snaked through her at his silky promise. She shut her mouth then because she wanted to enjoy the private serenade Darius Montagne was giving them in his raspy, husky tone.

Her gaze fell on Christian and Alessandra, who had joined them on the dance floor. Alessandra liked him, she knew, maybe more than liked the very stunning blond-haired investment genius. Yet they weren't looking at each other at all and Alessandra looked *miserable*.

She pushed back from Rocco, jerking her chin subtly in their direction. "Do you have any idea what's going on there?"

Rocco looked over at his sister. "She's been heartbroken without Giovanni. They were very close."

And maybe you are a blind, blind man. But Olivia wasn't about to stick her nose where it didn't belong. She'd caused enough waves today.

Rocco passed her to her father after that for a dance. What should have been extremely awkward given the little communication they'd had with each other over the past years was instead another kind of closure.

"You look happy with Ella," she said. "I'm glad."

"As do you with Rocco," he replied. "Liv, I…"

She shook her head. "It's okay, Dad. I understand. I do."

His eyes grew watery. "Sometimes you looked so much like her, it just…hurt to see you."

A fresh wave of tears pooled at the back of her eyes. She blinked them resolutely away. Sometimes life was heartbreaking. She saw that now. And sometimes you just had to forgive and move on.

"It's okay," she whispered, her hand tightening around her father's. "I'm glad you're here."

When she had made the requisite rounds of the dance floor with the rest of the Columbia Four, her husband stole her back for another dance. He, too, had taken some first baby steps with his father, the two of them having had a long talk while she'd been gone. It hadn't been perfect, but it was a start.

Rocco's warm, familiar scent wrapped itself around her as she tucked herself into his big warm body. She let most of the song go by before she drew back and looked up at him. "Rocco?"

His dark eyes, almost ebony tonight against the black tux, held hers. *"Sì?"*

"I'm not so interested in dancing. Do you mind if we skip it?"

He didn't bother to answer, just wrapped his hand around hers and pulled her through the dancers and up the two flights of stairs to their suite.

The windows were open as he worked the buttons on the back of her dress free. Darius Montagne's sexy rasp floated on the air up to them. Rocco's curse as his fingers fumbled over the tiny buttons made her smile.

"Mario again."

He continued doggedly, until he had most of them undone, then pushed the dress off her shoulders to fall in a pool of silk in the moonlight. She disposed of his jacket, shirt and tie as fast as her hands could move. Impatient with her lack of speed, even at the rate she was going, Rocco undid his belt and pushed the rest of his clothes off until there was only his magnificent, olive-skinned body to ogle.

He didn't give her much of a chance to do so, swinging her up into his arms and depositing her on the rose petal–covered bed. He took his time, lavishing every centimeter of her body with sensuous kisses until she was arching up against him, begging for his possession. His name a soft cry on her lips, he slid his hand between her thighs, prepared her for him and brought the tip of his impressive erection exactly where she needed him.

"Ti amo," he murmured as he possessed her body and

soul. He said it over and over again, as if he couldn't say it enough, until his kiss captured her scream and forever with him was all she could see.

I love you, too, my dragon slayer. She wound her arms around his neck and laid her face against his chest. Because sometimes you needed to fight your own battles, and sometimes you needed a warrior to help you along your way.

* * * * *

Look out for the next installment of
SOCIETY WEDDINGS:
THE GREEK'S PREGNANT BRIDE
by Michelle Smart
Coming next month!

New York Fashion Confidential

Antonia Vanelli

THE HOUSE OF MONDELLI returned to the stage Thursday night with New York Fashion Week's most talked-about fall/winter collection, silencing speculation the venerable Italian fashion house would falter in the wake of the death of its brilliant founder, Giovanni Mondelli. The company made a clear statement that a succession plan has long been in place with the debut of three sensational new young designers who knocked our socks off with their innovative, hip vibe.

The new designers, led by veteran Mario Masini, showcased a fresh, youthful direction for Mondelli that many felt it had been sorely lacking. Their off-bias, irreverent collection in muted colors for fall was by far the highlight of a week devoted to what seemed like exhaustive replays of years gone past.

The show also offered the highlight moment of the week for fashiongoers—the return of one of the world's most famous supermodels, Olivia Fitzgerald, to headline the night. With the plethora of new talent on display, one would think attention would have been squarely focused on the clothes, but word has it the action backstage was even more compelling.

The rumor mill has been off the charts since Fitzgerald announced her return to modeling after reneging on a

three-million-dollar contract with French cosmetics man-
ufacturer Le Ciel and disappearing into thin air last year,
leaving boyfriend and noted fashion photographer Guillermo Villanueva brokenhearted. The announcement of
Fitzgerald's engagement to Mondelli CEO Rocco Mondelli took many off guard, particularly, my sources tell
me, heartthrob Villanueva. Villanueva has not been seen
on the arm of a female since his breakup with Fitzgerald,
and Thursday night might just have proved why.

Sources backstage say the first meeting between
Fitzgerald and Villanueva since the announcement of
her engagement was a tense, bittersweet moment with all
signs pointing to the fact the swarthy, Venezuelan-born
photographer is still in love with his former muse. Given
Fitzgerald is now engaged to dark and dangerous Mondelli, previously considered an uncatchable target, there
was bound to be tension. The two men apparently managed to avoid each other until Fitzgerald suffered an apparent panic attack prior to going onstage and was talked
through it by Mondelli.

Fitzgerald came offstage "white as a ghost and visibly
shaken," says my source, after a performance that was
wobbly and not at all like her vintage self. "Fitzgerald's
two beaux were poised to comfort her, causing a most
uncomfortable moment." Villanueva evidently ended up
without the girl. No doubt the ladies are poised to line up
to console the charismatic photographer now that his period of mourning has officially been put to rest.

"Fitzgerald and Mondelli are obviously very much in
love," said the source, who speculated a panic attack was
also the cause of Fitzgerald's nonappearance in the show
last year. "But one has to wonder, with a performance that
shaky, if Mondelli's investment in Fitzgerald on the business side was a wise one."

This fashion veteran, for one, hopes it will be. I've always loved the way Olivia Fitzgerald commands a catwalk. She is one of the few women in the world who can put on a coat and convince you that you must have it immediately, and I'm looking forward to her next appearance in London and to that swagger of hers making a return to the stage.

As for the delicious Guillermo Villanueva…? We'll keep you posted.

Read on for a SOCIETY WEDDINGS Exclusive!

Rocco & Olivia's wedding day through the eyes of
Stefan Bianco

STEFAN BIANCO HAD always considered himself a man above
trite, clichéd expressions, but in Olivia Fitzgerald's case,
his first impression had indeed been worth a thousand
words.

The night he and the couple had celebrated Olivia and
Rocco's engagement at his restaurant Tempesta Di Fuoco
in Chelsea, he had watched with a mixture of horror and
amusement as the legendary blonde beauty had dismantled
his ultracool, unruffled friend in front of his eyes, turning
the notorious bachelor into a bewitched specimen of manhood none of the Columbia Four would have recognized
if they'd been there to witness it.

At the time Stefan had laughed it off, thinking this was
Rocco's bed, and if he wanted to make it with the stunning, former supermodel Olivia, who was he to voice an
objection? It had been a brilliant strategic choice on Rocco's part to wed one of the world's most recognizable faces
and send the Mondelli brand skyrocketing. But the way
his friend had been acting?

Of all the four men who'd attended Columbia University together and bonded into an inviolate brotherhood
dubbed the Columbia Four—himself, Sheikh Zayed Al
Afzal, Christian Markos and Rocco Mondelli—Rocco had

been the toughest. The hardest. Behind himself, of course. But he was a special case...

At Columbia they'd joked Rocco was aptly named for his impenetrable heart. For his lack of emotion in sending yet another female to the curb when he was no longer interested... Yet here he was on his wedding day, calmly sweating it out as he waited for his bride to appear like an apparition sent from the gods above to save his breaking soul.

If she loves me, she'll come.

Stefan shoved his hands in his pockets to prevent them from shaking some sense into Rocco as that fatalistic drivel continued to spew out of his friend's mouth. Olivia wasn't here to throttle. He would have enjoyed that.

Rocco's bride was missing.

Oh, she was somewhere in Italy, to be sure. They'd learned that this morning when she'd landed at the Milan airport at eleven. But given the argument she and Rocco had apparently had, the subject matter of which Rocco refused to divulge, Olivia's appearance in Lake Como at the Mondellis' historic family villa for the society wedding of the decade was not at all a given.

"I'm going to drive into Milan and check the apartment," Rocco announced. "Olivia loves the gardens there. It's a possibility."

"It's also a possibility she might use her phone," Stefan exploded, abandoning his pockets to throw his hands in the air.

Rocco gave Stefan a hard look. "Stay here with Zayed and keep things running. Make sure what needs to happen happens. You," Rocco said, tossing his car keys at Christian, "drive."

Stefan watched with slack-jawed amazement as Rocco and Christian jogged down the front steps of Villa Mondelli, across the lawn teeming with caterers and wedding staff and toward the car park. His tux jacket and tie discarded, his gaze tunnel-visioned, Rocco had the glazed look of a man on the edge.

And now he was leaving the site where five hundred people were gathering in just under three hours for his nuptials in the hopes of finding his fiancée *sniffing a rosebush*?

"Someone needs to stop him," Stefan muttered. "Someone needs to stop *this*."

"He's pursuing his destiny," Zayed murmured. "Leave the man to it."

Rage, pure unadorned rage that had been building up inside Stefan all morning, a rage he knew to be about more than this, about the subject of women leaving in general, bubbled up inside of him until it spilled out of his lips in a harsh, unavoidable attack.

"Did you *actually* just say that?"

Zayed turned his dark, dark eyes on him, armed with that Zen thing he did so well. "We're all concerned about Rocco, Stefan. But the man knows his mind. He knows *this*. So stop projecting your anger on the situation and use the opportunity to examine where it's coming from."

Stefan felt the jab right through him. It knocked the breath from him, his coiled fingers swinging uselessly by his sides. Then he recovered without acknowledging the truth or error of Zayed's statement, gave his friend the most disgusted look he could manage and walked away.

Zayed could stand there doing nothing while Rocco flailed. *He* had to do something. He was Sicilian. He had been bred to make things happen. Or make things not happen, in this case. And he needed the madness to stop.

He was midway through his third phone call, this time to a friend in the local police department, when Zayed informed him Olivia and her mother had just pulled up in the car park. Pocketing his mobile, he pushed the other man's arm aside, took the steps to the lawn two by two and headed for satisfaction.

Olivia stood by a small compact car alongside what had to be her mother given the likeness in resemblance. The wedding planner was with them, barking orders with the relieved expression of a woman who'd escaped a death sentence. Except now she had to get the groom back here in time.

Stefan stopped in front of Olivia, as tall, lanky and stunning as ever, steam coming out of his ears.

"How *could* you?" he bit out.

Olivia whitened. Her mother went to stand between them, but Olivia brushed her mother's arm aside and lifted her chin. The vulnerability painted across her face, the dark, haunted shadows underneath her signature blue eyes, stopped his anger in its tracks.

"I'm sorry," she said quietly. "I needed to make sure I was doing the right thing."

It floored him for a moment, the honesty. How miserable she looked… How the complexity of what she and Rocco shared was written across her uncertain face.

"I love him." She said the words tentatively at first, then with greater force. "I love him, Stefan. Madly. Deeply."

The veracity of her confession reached down to his jaded, black heart. Felled him on the spot.

"Lucky for you, Olivia Fitzgerald," he said harshly. "You just said the only three words that matter."